"We'll have our talk in the card room."

"No!" The exclamation bubbled almost hysterically from Kelly's throat. She didn't want to go anywhere with this man. The room would be empty and there would be an intimacy that she could not endure.

"Yes," was Nicholas's impatient command. "Your offer of help interests me. The spoiled rich girl wishes to make amends by playing Lady Bountiful...."

"No need to make it sound so ugly," Kelly protested. "I merely want to help."

"In order to ease your conscience with money? Tell me, Miss Stanwick, do you buy your way out of every unpleasant situation?"

Kelly was stung. She was *not* mercenary at all—but she would give any amount of money to escape from the contemptuous presence of Nicholas Van Mijden!

Other titles by

ROSEMARY
CARTER
IN HARLEQUIN PRESENTS

ADAM'S BRIDE 263
SWEET IMPOSTER 283
BUSH DOCTOR 290
THE AWAKENING 301
MY DARLING SPITFIRE 337

Other titles by

ROSEMARY
CARTER
IN HARLEQUIN ROMANCES

MAN OF THE WILD 1986
RETURN TO DEVIL'S VIEW 2312

Many of these titles, and other titles in the Harlequin
Romance series, are available at your local book-
seller. For a free catalogue listing all available
Harlequin Presents and Harlequin Romances, send
your name and address to:

HARLEQUIN READER SERVICE,
M.P.O. Box 707,
Niagara Falls, N.Y. 14302

Canadian address:
Stratford, Ontario, Canada N5A 6W2

ROSEMARY CARTER

kelly's man

Harlequin Books

TORONTO · LONDON · NEW YORK · AMSTERDAM
SYDNEY · HAMBURG · PARIS · STOCKHOLM

Harlequin Presents edition published June 1980
ISBN 0-373-10362-X

Original Hardcover edition published in 1980
by Mills & Boon Limited

CHAPTER ONE

'FOR the last time, George—will you take us up to Berg tomorrow?'

'No, Mr Sloan. I told you, it isn't safe. The trail is still too slippery after the rain.'

For a few moments there was silence. Looking from one face to another, Kelly did not know then that it was a scene which she would remember long afterwards. Gary Sloan, her fiancé, his good-looking face flushed and defiant. George Anderson, proprietor of Great Peaks Lodge, standing his ground, yet uncomfortable because his guests were displeased. Sheila and Alex, interested bystanders, eager to follow the trail but, unlike their friend, with nothing at stake.

And a little apart, watching the scene with an expression that was at once aloof and sardonic, a tall rugged-featured man whom Kelly had heard addressed only as Nicholas.

'Then I'll go alone.' Gary spoke into the silence, his voice a little too loud, his eyes blazing with recklessness.

'No, Gary!' She drew a taut breath as she put a detaining hand on her fiancé's arm. 'You can't!'

'Try stopping me.' Sullenly he pushed her hand away. Briefly Kelly was reminded of a little boy who had been thwarted in a game. Then he said, 'I *must* take a picture from the overhanging rock. You

know there's a sizeable bet on it,' and she realised
the analogy had been incorrect. Gary had gambled
more than he could afford, and he was grimly determined not to lose the bet.

There were times when Kelly wondered how well
she knew her fiancé. Their courtship had been so
much a whirlwind affair that there had been little
time to learn much of each other's essential char-
acters. Yet already she had come to recognise a
streak of daring and recklessness, a determination
to have his own way no matter the cost. But while
she was fascinated by this side of his nature—until
now she had never known anyone quite like Gary—
she was frightened by it too.

She had felt the tautness in his arm. He had to
do what he wanted. Nothing could stand in his
way. He had made a bet that he would take a photo
of the overhanging rock, and it was a bet he meant
to win, no matter the danger. And there *was*
danger in taking the trail without a guide, Kelly
knew; perhaps more than Gary cared to think
about. In the circumstances, there was only one
thing to do: George Anderson must be persuaded
to be their guide.

'Mr Anderson, won't you think about it?' She
smiled at him, warmth lighting green eyes fringed
with long black lashes. Kelly, who knew only the
image her mirror threw back at her, was unaware
that her eyes danced when she smiled, or that her
lips curved appealingly, so that she looked somehow vulnerable and younger than her twenty-three
years. But if there were those who melted to her
smile, the hotel-keeper stood his ground.

'I can't do it,' he muttered unhappily.

Another glance at Gary. Both hands were stuck in the pockets of his corded trousers. A mutinous look had been added to the recklessness in his eyes. There was no hint of softening, of giving in . . .

Kelly took a deep breath. She hated to use her money to gain an advantage for herself, but for once it seemed necessary. There was Gary's safety to consider. Besides, George Anderson had an air of solid reliability which was reassuring. He might not like the situation, but she did not doubt that he could cope with it. 'We would make it worth your while,' she said.

A stir of interest. All eyes swung to Kelly's face. Though her attention at that moment should have been solely on George's reaction, inexplicably her gaze was drawn to Nicholas, the stern-faced man who nursed his beer at the next table. His eyes had narrowed, his expression was derisive. Kelly felt warmth wash her cheeks.

She lifted her head and looked back at George. As steadily as she was able, she told him what she would pay him to take the group up the mountain.

'Miss Stanwick . . .' the first hint of unbending in the hotel-keeper's stance, 'I must think . . .'

'Don't be a fool, George.' The man called Nicholas spoke for the first time. His voice was hard.

George Anderson shifted restlessly. 'I do have to think, Nick . . . Most of the trail is okay.'

'Not near the rock. It's treacherous.'

'Sure. But I know that trail like the back of my hand.'

Nicholas turned and fixed Kelly with a scathing

glance. 'If it's the money, it's not worth it, George.'

'Look, Nick, you know how things are here right now.' The hotel-keeper was undecided, so obviously tempted by her offer that Kelly was ashamed. As she watched him her stomach muscles knotted with tension. But she did not withdraw the offer, for she knew the danger to Gary if he went up the mountain alone.

George said, 'Mary's expecting the baby in three months, and our finances....' He stared down at hands that worked nervously in his lap. Then he looked up and his face was set in the lines of a man who has made up his mind. 'I'll do it,' he said.

Kelly imagined that Nicholas would argue, that he would dredge up an argument to deflect George from his decision. But she had underestimated the tough self-sufficiency of the man. There was another hard look, one which raked her contemptuously, then he shrugged and addressed himself to the hotel-keeper. 'It's up to you.' He stood up, a long lean figure, tanned and muscled and with an air of polished steel. 'Be seeing you.'

'Then you'll really take us up?' Gary asked exultantly, when Nicholas had left the lounge.

'Yes.'

'Fantastic! We'll start first thing tomorrow morning.'

'It would be better to wait a day or two, give the ground a chance to dry...'

'No.' There was no hesitation in the younger man's tone. 'We want to move on the day after. No, George, old pal, we'll go tomorrow.'

Later, when they were alone together, Gary

pulled Kelly to him. 'Thanks, honey. Trust my darling fiancée to save the situation!'

She stirred restlessly in his arms, evading the breath that fanned a hot cheek, the lips that sought hers. 'I don't like it, Gary.'

He was amused. 'When we're married you'll have to learn not to be such an old stick-in-the-mud.'

'I hate bribing people,' she protested.

'For heaven's sake, Kelly!' Though he was laughing, she sensed his exasperation. 'You've done George a favour. He needs the money, you heard that. And I'll win my bet. Jeepers, Joe will be mad when he sees the pictures and has to pay up!' He held her away from him and looked down at her, his eyes glowing with an intense inner excitement. 'What shall we do with the money? Have ourselves a super deluxe party?'

'Do you think money exists only for enjoyment?' Her voice was troubled.

'Of course not.' He frowned impatiently. 'But there's no law that says you can't use some of it for pleasure. And you have so much, Kelly darling.'

She caught her breath, wondering if the words would have slipped out had he not been so exhilarated. Gary had made it clear from the start that the fact that her father was one of the richest industrialists in the country did not matter to him, and she believed him. Nevertheless, the words hit her dully, making her feel oddly depressed.

'Let's find Sheila and Alex,' she suggested, withdrawing from his arms.

It was apparent that he had noticed her mood, for he tried a moment longer to hold her against him. Then he shrugged. 'Let's,' he agreed. 'We need to make plans for tomorrow.'

They set out at daybreak next morning. All were warmly dressed, for dawn was a chilly time in the mountains of the Drakensberg. Dew lay heavy on the long rough grass, brushing against their clothes as they walked. Their spirits were high. Even Kelly had shed the depression which had been with her since the discussion in the hotel lounge the previous day. The mountain air had a freshness which was intoxicating, crisp and clean and aromatic with the scents of trees and wild flowers.

George seemed to have forgotten his earlier misgivings, or if he had not he did not mention them. He walked ahead with Gary and Alex. Gary had his camera slung around his neck, and Kelly could hear him telling the hotel-keeper of the bet he had made and why this particular set of photos was of such importance to him.

She could not hear all of his words, but his voice carried through the stillness, vital and excited and boyish. This was the Gary with whom she had fallen in love, impulsive and lively and fun to be with. An antidote to the staidness of a home where both parents were elderly and the guests they entertained were mainly business associates who were interested in the world of finance to an extent which made Kelly wonder sometimes if they had forgotten that there was more to life than just money.

Her parents had **not** been happy with her engagement—their visions of a future son-in-law had been of a man who had made his mark in the world

—but Kelly had been adamant that Gary was the man she wanted to marry, and eventually they had agreed to the engagement. The wedding was three months away, and already elaborate preparations were being made.

When Kelly had told her parents that she and Gary would be joining his friends Alex and Sheila for a fortnight's holiday in Natal and the mountains of the Drakensberg, she realised they were displeased. But they had not objected. For one thing, Kelly was old enough to lead her own life. For another, she had made it clear that she would be sharing a room with Sheila throughout. If her parents suspected that Gary might try to persuade her to share a room with him instead, they kept their suspicions to themselves. Kelly was twenty-three, and until now she had shown that she could look after herself.

Quite apart from her moral attitude to the matter —a morality which was part of her character, and which, she knew, Sheila and Alex and perhaps even Gary laughed at in private—there was another reason why Kelly would not have wanted to share a room with her fiancée. It was a reason which had to do with Gary himself. For though she was certain she loved him, there were times when he alarmed her, times when she was frightened by a sudden wildness or a totally unpredictable action. No, not frightened ... that was too strong a word. Perhaps after all alarm more aptly described her emotion. And a sense of doubt which she tried very hard to suppress. All of which was absurd, for it was his unorthodox nature which fascinated her, and which had led her to fall in love with him in the first place.

She was glad, Kelly told herself almost fiercely, that Gary had the courage to be different, that he did not kowtow to her as so many men had done in the past, merely because her father was very rich and she, as his only daughter, would one day inherit all he possessed. Nevertheless, there were times—like yesterday, when George Anderson had been persuaded into agreeing to his whims—when she wished that he would curb the streak that was not only wild but stubborn as well.

In refusing to share his bed at this stage, she was not only holding firm to her principles, she was also giving herself a chance to come to terms with Gary as a person, a husband, a man whom she would love not only for the aspects of his personality which appealed to her, but also those which, initially, were foreign to her.

Involuntarily, and without good reason, her mind went to the rugged-faced man called Nicholas. He had made no attempt to hide his contempt at the scene in the lounge. She remembered the arrogant lift of the strong eyebrows, the derision in the grey eyes. She remembered also the look of steel and virility that seemed as much a part of him as the long muscled body and stern tanned features. The thought of him was enough to make her stiffen with tension. The fact that she had taken an instant dislike to the man was no reason to let him interfere with the enjoyment of this day, she told herself angrily. Yet the effort it took to push him from her mind was surprising.

In the light of early dawn the mountains had been grey and brooding, a shadowed mass of towering lines. Now the sun was rising, and with it the countryside was suddenly transformed. The blur of shapes separated into mountains with distinguishable form and shape. It grew lighter, warmer, and by the time George signalled that it was time to stop for breakfast, each member of the party was ready to shed an outer jacket.

George carried a haversack with provisions. After coffee that was strong and steaming, and some sandwiches, they moved on. As the sun climbed higher in the sky, Kelly was struck by the sheer beauty all around her. There was the majesty of the Drakensberg escarpment, one mountain unfolding behind another in a range that ran as far as the eyes could see and beyond. Dragon mountains, as was suggested by their name ... There was the loveliness of the veld, green and fresh after the recent rains, and colourful with thousands of tiny wild flowers. Here and there were bushes with aloes and proteas, the waxy cactus-shaped flowers which were as much a part of Africa as the thorny acacias and the long rough grass of the bush. The air rang with the sound of bird-song, and once a widow-bird crossed the path, flying very near to the ground, with its long widow-weed tail trailing cumbrously behind it. And always there was the sound of water, unusual in a country where rivers and lakes were a rarity. Streams cascaded down the granite slopes of the mountains, rippling and gurgling over rocks, the water clear and inviting. George told Kelly that the streams were the tributaries of a river which flowed through the farmlands of Natal until it reached the sea.

The trail began to climb the side of a mountain. The going was not always easy, for the ground was slippery as George had warned. Now and then it wound uncomfortably close to the edge of a cliff, and often the long veld grass obscured its direction for quite some distance. Clearly it was a trail that only experienced hikers would take on their own. As she followed George's wide back, Kelly was glad that they were not attempting the excursion without a guide.

After a while they entered a canyon. Kelly sensed Gary's mounting excitement. The overhanging rock could not be far away. Now the mountains were tall and dark and very close on all sides. Kelly had not realised quite how high they had climbed until she looked down and saw the floor of the canyon far below. Trees, spindly and leafless, stuck out from the cliff-side at odd angles, their roots sprawling like gaunt octopus tentacles over the bare rocks, and a stream, like a thin silver thread, snaked its way between the canyon walls.

It was almost midday when they came at last to the rock. Kelly drew in her breath at the sight of it. It was flat and long, protruding quite some way beyond the sheer edge of the cliff, with nothing but space for thousands of feet beneath it.

The path was very near the edge of the cliff, and Kelly felt a sudden wave of dizziness. Her legs went weak, and the colour drained from her face. In his excitement at having reached the rock, Gary did not notice her distress, but George did. He put a quick arm around her waist to support her, then he propelled her backwards to a point where she could lean against the slope of a sandy bank.

With exclamations of boyish glee Gary and Alex walked on to the rock. Kelly wanted to call out a warning, to beg them to remain where they were, but she stifled the words. She knew her fiancé well enough to know that he had not come so far just to stay on the path. She was relieved when George joined them on the rock. He would keep the two young men from doing anything foolish.

Gary took his camera from his shoulder and began to take pictures, and watching him, Kelly began to relax. Even without George beside him she could see that he was steady and unafraid. They had come all this way without incident. When Gary had his pictures they would go back the way they had come. Tomorrow they would be leaving the Drakensberg. Gary would have the completed film in his suitcase and would be elated at the prospect of winning his bet. She wondered now why she had been quite so tense.

The men left the rock and came back to the path. George was chuckling quietly in response to something Alex had said, while Gary was flushed with achievement.

'Glad you came?' Kelly smiled up at her fiancé.

'It was great up there.' His eyes shone with excitement. 'You should have come—Sheila too. It was a fantastic experience!'

Kelly laughed as she shook her head. 'I don't have your courage. But I'm glad you have all your pictures.'

'All but one.' Gary shot a swift glance at George who was still talking to Alex, and then without a word he left the edge of the path and made to climb a little way down the slope. Evidently he wanted a picture of the rock from a different angle.

'Gary! Don't!' The protest burst tautly from Kelly's throat.

George spun round, caught by the horror in her voice.

'Get back immediately!' The command rang out, sharp and angry.

'Don't panic.' Gary's voice floated up to them, cool and amused. 'Just this one picture and then....'

The words slid into a scream of terror. Then came the appalling sound of a fall.

Kelly opened her mouth, but her mouth was so dry that no words came. Her eyes were closed and she was shuddering violently, sick with horror and shock at the thought of the handsome young body lying broken on the floor of the canyon.

'Kelly!' Dimly, through the thudding in her temples, she heard George's voice, felt his hand on her arm. 'Gary's okay.' And then, more impatiently, 'Look after her, Sheila. She looks as if she could faint and I don't want another casualty on my hands. I'm going after Gary.'

'You mean....' She was still shivering as she opened her eyes and tried to focus. 'Gary ... he isn't...?'

'He fell on to a ledge.' Alex sounded subdued and frightened. 'But he can't get back. George is going down to get him.'

It was quite still on the path at the edge of the cliff. Not a word was exchanged between the three people who stood watching, waiting. There was only the fierceness of the sun, almost at its zenith in the vastness of the African sky, and the closeness of the mountains, a closeness that was suddenly menacing. The only sounds came from below them, where a drama of life and death was being played out on a narrow strip of rock; there was the snapping of a branch, the nerve-rendering skitter of a stone, a groan.

It soon became evident that Gary had lost his nerve, and that George was having to manipulate him back up the slope. There was a simultaneous expelling of breath as a fair head showed above the level of the path. Even then Gary could not manage the remaining few feet on his own. Alex reached him a hand and pulled him on to the path, where he sank down, exhausted.

Kelly was about to kneel at his side when it happened. A rock was dislodged by Gary's foot. George dodged its fall. It missed his head, but struck his leg. An exclamation of pain, and then George had slipped back on to the ledge.

The next hours were a nightmare Kelly would never forget. Kelly and Sheila remained on the cliff path by the overhanging rock while Gary and Alex went back to the hotel to seek help. The two girls were unable to go down to George. There was the danger that in their inexperience they too would slip, and this time the ledge might not stop a fall. They could only stay where they were, and call words of encouragement down the slope. After a while George ceased to answer. They knew already that his leg had been injured by the falling rock, and that he was in great pain. They did not know the extent of the injury, and when he lapsed into silence they could only guess he was unconscious. There was nothing they could do but pray that he would lie still until help came.

There was little communication between the two girls. Kelly had been aware of Sheila's antagonism from the start; an antagonism that stemmed—judging by her comments—from envy of Kelly's money. Till now the antagonism had been veiled with a kind of joking asperity. Once Kelly had mentioned it to Gary, but he had said she was over-sensitive, imagining something that did not exist. Although she did not agree with him, Kelly had not mentioned the matter again. She had in fact tried to get on with the other girl, because if she had allowed an argument to flare up between them, it would have become impossible for them to share a room. At times Kelly suspected that this was just what Sheila wanted, for she had made it quite clear that she had expected to sleep with Alex. So Kelly, to whom the status quo was important, had done her best to keep the relationship harmonious, at least on the surface.

Now, with George unconscious beneath them, there was silence on the cliff path. For once Kelly made no attempt to be friendly. It was as if the starkness of the accident had shown the futility of sham smiles and small-talk, had stripped away the differences between reality and pretence. It was a starkness which demanded honesty, which defied any effort at pushing unpleasant thoughts to the further reaches of the mind.

Sitting on the rough scrub, with only a stunted acacia for shade, Kelly was forced to assess what had happened. In particular she was forced to think of her fiancé as he had revealed himself in the last twenty-four hours. She was forced to admit that the recklessness and impetuousness which had appealed to her were in fact parts of a personality in which selfishness yielded to nothing.

For she had seen Gary's face when he had left the overhanging rock with Alex. For a short while after he had reached the sanctuary of the path he had been confused, uncertain, glad to have firm ground beneath his feet. There had been a look in his eyes which revealed that there had been a few moments when the threat of death had been very real.

It was a look which lasted no more than minutes. By the time he left with Alex to go back along the way they had come, the old expression was in his eyes—the wildness, the daring. And something more—a stormy defiance, the resentment of one who was being made, against his will, to pay the price for his misdeeds.

In vain Kelly had searched his face for a hint of remorse.

Was this the real Gary? she wondered now, as the long slumbrous afternoon hours merged one into another. All the qualities which had once seemed so attractive, were they no more than the trappings of a man who was wilful and stubborn to the exclusion of anyone but himself?

Thoughtfully she looked at the ring which sparked blue fire on the third finger of her left hand. Was it only the accident which made her so introspective, so that she felt she was engaged to a stranger whom she knew hardly at all?

It came to her quite suddenly that she loved Gary. Loving a person meant accepting his good points along with the bad. She had her own imperfections. How would she feel if Gary stopped loving her merely because her behaviour did not meet his expectations? Besides, she was engaged to him; she had made a commitment. And having made a commitment Kelly did not easily retreat.

The afternoon moved on. Shadows formed, lengthened. Now and then Kelly walked a little way back along the path to a point where she could see some distance out of the mountain cleft and into the valley where the hotel was situated, but nothing stirred. Anxiously she looked down the slope. George was still motionless. She hoped he would remain so, for a returning consciousness would bring pain and the dreadful danger that he would move and fall from the ledge.

But there was danger also in his unconsciousness. As hot as it had been during the day, Kelly knew that once the sun set it would grow cold very quickly. She and Sheila had their cardigans; they could even huddle together if it grew really cold. But George wore only shorts and a cotton shirt. He could die of exposure. If only they could find a way of keeping him warm . . .

She glanced at Sheila, who was leaning back on

her elbows, her expression remote. 'I hope the men reached the hotel safely.'

'Alex will certainly hear from me if they dawdled.'

'Do you think...' It was hard to say the words, when the implications of the question were so serious. 'Do you think the rescue party will find its way in the dark?'

'They'd better.' Sheila's voice was hard. 'I have no intention of spending the night in this God-forsaken spot.'

'You don't care about George, do you?' The words were out before Kelly could stop them, her dislike of the other girl so intense that she forgot her resolve to be tactful. 'He could die of exposure.'

'He knew the risks when he took your money.' There was no mistaking the malice in Sheila's tone, nor the emphasis on the word 'your'. She went on before Kelly could speak, 'And don't pretend to be so shocked. You knew what you were doing when you bribed him.'

Kelly bit back the retort which sprang to her lips. It was futile to argue. Sickened, she looked away into the growing darkness.

It was dark when the rescue party arrived, an eerie darkness, with just a narrow wedge of star-studded sky visible in the cleft between the mountains rising high on both sides of the canyon. Kelly breathed with relief at the first sight of flickering torchlight.

It was another half hour before the rescuers finally came to the rock. Gary and Alex were with the party, but it was the man called Nicholas who

claimed Kelly's startled attention. He did not speak
to the girls, except to ask them a few necessary
questions. Then he began to direct the rescue operations. As Kelly watched him, she was caught by his
air of authority and a decisiveness that was sure
without being over-confident. She did not know
who the men were who comprised the rescue party,
but she saw that they worked as a team, looking to
Nicholas as their leader, accepting his orders without question.

Though the operation was fraught with danger,
there was no sense of panic. It was as if the team
knew that the man who led them would make the
wisest decisions possible in the circumstances, that
he would do what had to be done without creat-
ing unnecessary hazards. Kelly knew how they felt
because she felt the same way, though she could not
have explained the reason.

Nicholas was more than a man who gave direc-
tives. Kelly watched him climb down the slope to the
ledge where George lay. She was not consciously
aware that she was holding her breath, that his
safety was in some peculiar way important to her.
But when George was hauled at last to safety, and
when Nicholas reached the cliff path once more
she was filled with relief—also an inexplicable pride.

George was laid gently on a stretcher and covered
with blankets. He stirred once and groaned, and
Kelly wondered if he was coming round. Then he
lay still again and she was glad. The way down the
mountain would be bumpy. Better for George to
be unconscious than to suffer extra pain.

As the rescue party started on its way Nicholas

looked at Kelly. There was nothing casual in the glance. It excluded Sheila, even Gary and Alex who had watched the entire proceedings silently and without any offer of help. It was a hard look, loaded with unspoken contempt. It was an effort to meet that look, but somehow Kelly managed it. The silent interchange lasted no more than a few seconds. But inside Kelly, as she began to follow the swaying stretcher with her fiancé and his friends, tension formed a tight knot of pain.

CHAPTER TWO

When Kelly awoke the next morning she dressed quickly and went to the office. She learned that George had been taken to hospital and that Mary, his wife, was with him. Nothing was known yet of his condition, except that it seemed likely that his leg was broken. It seemed there was nothing she could do except to ask the desk clerk to convey her regrets for the accident as well as her best wishes. She would have liked to remain at the hotel a while longer, at least until there was more definite news of George, but even last night, as they had walked wearily back to the hotel through the darkness, Gary had been adamant about leaving. Nothing would induce him to change his mind. Alex and Sheila felt the same way.

There was no sign of Nicholas in the dining-room or in the grounds of the hotel, and Kelly told herself that she was glad. His contempt as they had begun the walk down the mountain was still very vivid in her mind.

Breakfast was an uncomfortable meal, hasty and tasteless. It was as if Gary, Alex and Sheila could not wait to go. When they had finished eating the men bundled the suitcases into the car. As they drove down the long winding path that led from Great Peaks Lodge to the main road, Kelly noticed that none of her companions turned back to the hotel for a last look.

They had been out of the mountains for some hours now. The countryside was less dramatic but still beautiful, green and gently undulating in a manner very typical of Natal, but Kelly saw none of it.

'We ought to go back,' she observed.

'That's the fourth time you've said it.' Gary was impatient. 'You're beginning to sound boring.'

Alex and Sheila said nothing, but they had made their comments already. Kelly knew that they felt as Gary did; George Anderson had known what he was doing when he had agreed to guide them up the mountain. The accident had been unfortunate, but they were in no way to blame. As far as they were concerned the matter was ended.

'George didn't know you would go down the slope.' Kelly bit her lip, knowing the remark would incur her fiancé's anger. 'He tried to call you back.'

'Give me a break, Kelly!' The hands that clenched the wheel were white-knuckled, the eyes that turned momentarily from the road blazed with uncontrolled fury. 'I didn't mean to slip. None of us are perfect.' He paused. When he went on his tone was edged with malice. 'Though perhaps having so much money gives you an illusion of perfection.'

A hushed silence followed his words. Kelly stared at Gary as if at a stranger. Every nerve quivered with anger and disappointment. Words rushed to her lips, but she bit them back as something inside her urged her to keep silent, telling her to leave further discussion of what had happened until a time when emotions had cooled. This was only the first crisis in her life with Gary. There would be others. Unless she learned how to deal with them there could be no happiness in their marriage.

And then she knew that she could not keep silent, no matter the consequences. In a tight voice she said, 'When we get to Estcourt you can drop me at the station.'

'Honey...' There was a new look in Gary's eyes, one which Kelly wished she had not seen. It was a look which was oddly out of place in her exuberant fiancé, as if he was seeing a prize vanishing from his fingers and wondered what he could do to prevent it happening. His voice too held an unaccustomed note of panicked conciliation. 'Look, honey, perhaps I've been a bit hard, but...'

She could not bear to hear any more. She did not want to see Gary debase himself. 'Leave it now.' She forced a smile. 'I'll take a railway coach back to the hotel. I want to make sure George is all right.'

'We could all go...'

'No.' She shook her head a little too firmly. More than anything else she needed to be on her own for a while. 'I'll meet up with you in Durban. No, Gary, please don't say anything more. I'm going back alone.'

The desk clerk looked only mildly surprised to see her. In response to Kelly's question, he said that he thought Mrs Anderson was resting; she had spent most of the night at the hospital.

A little disconsolately Kelly turned away. She

had returned to Great Peaks Lodge with the purpose of seeing Mary Anderson. She still would see her. But for the moment she was uncertain what to do next. It did not occur to her to ask for a room. After she had spoken to George's wife she would make her way back to Estcourt and from there to Durban.

She walked a little way from the desk in the direction of the big french doors which led on to a wide verandah. Sooner or later, she supposed, Mary Anderson would emerge from her room. Then she would talk to her. In the meantime, it seemed there was nothing to do but stroll around the garden a while and enjoy the view of the mountains.

'Well, if it isn't Miss Stanwick!'

Kelly spun round. Lost in thought, she had not seen him approach. He was looking down at her, hands stuck carelessly in the waistband of well-tailored cord trousers, grey eyes narrowed and watchful. She knew his full name now—Nicholas Van Mijden. Irrelevantly it came to her that no man had the right to look quite as virile and masculine as he did.

She swallowed. 'Hello, Mr Van Mijden.'

'I understand you and your friends had left.'

'We had. I . . . I decided to come back.'

'Why?'

For somebody who, it seemed, must be employed at the hotel—hard though it was to see Nicholas Van Mijden accountable to anyone but himself—there was an arrogance in his tone towards a guest which was surely inappropriate.

He was waiting for her answer. For a moment she was tempted to turn her back on him. Then she thought better of it. The memory of his contempt on the mountain had in no way faded. For some reason she needed to redeem his impression of her. It did not occur to her at that moment why this should in any way be important.

'I'd like to help,' she said simply.

His eyes held hers steadily. 'Interesting,' he murmured without expression.

Kelly could have left it at that. Her business was with Mary Anderson, nobody else. But the direct gaze of the steady grey eyes was doing peculiar things to her heartbeat. She was filled with the sudden need to talk, anything to lessen the tension that was building inside her.

'I'll be speaking to Mrs Anderson.'

'Mary is resting. In the meantime, I'd like to hear about this offer myself.' He gestured. 'We'll talk in the card-room.'

'No!' The exclamation bubbled hysterically from her throat. She knew the card-room. She could not go there with this man. It would be empty at this time of the day, and she did not want to be alone with him. Not that he would harm her in any way, but there would be an intimacy, even if only she herself was aware of it, which she could not endure.

'Yes.' An impatient command. A hand gripped her arm, as if he meant to force her to go with him to the little room near the office. When she could catch her breath she would resent his autocratic manner. But for a moment there was only the tingling feeling on her skin where the lean fingers held her.

Abruptly she shook herself free. 'All right,' she agreed jerkily, 'though it's really no business of yours.'

'Where's Mr Sloan?' came the unexpected question, when the door of the little room was closed.

Kelly's chin lifted defiantly at his tone. There was no reason for this insufferable man to know the truth. 'He had to get back to Durban.'

'Leaving his fiancée to make amends on her own.' She saw the gleam in the dark eyes as he cut off her protest. 'Don't bother to defend him. What interests me is your own offer of help.'

For a few seconds she toyed with the idea of remaining silent. But there was something about this man—the tall broad shoulders blocking the doorway, the inherent sense of unyielding authority—which seemed to demand an answer.

'I intend to give Mrs Anderson some money.'

'Really?' he drawled, and it came to her that he was in no way surprised. 'So you've come back to play Lady Bountiful?'

'No need to make it sound so ugly!' She threw the words at him tightly. 'I had the feeling it might be of help.'

'Because you remembered George saying that money would be useful right now.' There was an ominous quality in the quiet voice.

'Well, yes...'

'Tell me, Miss Stanwick, do you buy your way out of every situation?'

She was stung by the deliberate insult. 'How dare you!' she exclaimed angrily.

He laughed mockingly. 'You don't like the truth?' A slight pause. 'Or is it just that your tribe of hangers-on tell you only what you want to hear?'

Anger surged through her, but even through the anger his words had the power to hurt. 'I don't care for your implications, Mr Van Mijden.' Somehow she managed to keep her voice low and controlled.

'No?' His gaze lingered on her face, taking in the stormy eyes, the flushed cheeks. Then it descended slowly, blatantly, to the intensely feminine curves of her figure. 'Perhaps it's just that as you're the only daughter of a millionaire industrialist none of your other acquaintances has ever thwarted you?'

She was shaken. He knew more about her than she had realised.

'I didn't think my father's name had spread this far.' She tried to keep her tone light.

'We do read newspapers in the backwaters of the Drakensberg.' There was a sardonic light in the glance he threw her. 'Even without that—there was the gossip of your friends.'

She looked at him, feeling a little sick. Whatever other faults her fiancé might have, surely he had not stooped to discussing her father's position? Nicholas Van Mijden seemed to sense the unspoken question, and unexpectedly there was a slight softening in the hard face. But it was a softness which did not extend to his words. 'You might have found their comments enlightening.'

Kelly found her voice. 'I don't believe you. Gary ... My fiancé wouldn't stoop to gossip.'

A shrug of broad shoulders. 'What you believe is

of no concern to me. But to get back to my original question—you *do* believe that money is the solution to all your problems, don't you?'

She made an effort to meet his eyes. When that became difficult her glance slipped to the well-shaped nose, the mobile lips, the strong sweep of the jaw. If he was not handsome in a conventional sense his air of uncompromising maleness and toughness nonetheless made him the most arresting man she had ever encountered. He was also rude and arrogant and lacking in manners. In fact he possessed all the qualities she most detested.

'You're referring to the payment I offered George yesterday,' she said at last, with as much composure as she could muster.

'Offer of payment,' he jeered. 'A spade is a spade, Miss Stanwick, and a bribe is a bribe in any language.'

She felt the colour rise in her cheeks. It was becoming hard to breathe. It was as if the tall broad-shouldered figure took up most of the space in the room, though she knew, logically, that this could not be so.

There was truth in what he said. But it was not the whole truth. She *had* offered the money as an inducement, but she had not meant it as a bribe. She had seen it only as a way of averting an accident, never dreaming that an accident of another sort would happen in consequence.

'I don't expect you to understand,' she began uncertainly, then stopped. It was hard to explain her motivation, without in some way indicting Gary. He was reckless, even selfish perhaps. But she wore his ring, and had promised to be his wife, and she owed him some loyalty. A small pink tongue went out to moisten a dry lower lip. 'The photo was of great importance to my fiancé.'

'So important that all safety precautions could be disregarded. No,' he said in a hard voice, 'I don't understand.'

How clever he was at making her feel small! But not so clever that he did not see the only fallacy in his accusations.

'Assuming it was a bribe—which I dispute—why did George accept? He could have remained firm in his refusal.'

Something came and went in the grey eyes, and a muscle tightened in the long line of the jaw. 'You heard George say the money would be useful. The Andersons have been through a bad patch, and Mary's baby is due soon. You caught George at a very low moment, Miss Stanwick.'

'I see...' She kept her expression composed, but deep inside her there was a stab of shame and compassion. Then she said, 'That being the case, Mr Van Mijden, why do you object to the fact that I want to help?'

An eyebrow lifted. 'Did I say I object?'

She stared at him uncertainly, wondering that he had the power to make her feel quite so vulnerable. 'Isn't that what all the sarcasm is about?'

'You *have* misunderstood.' He chuckled, and the sound was low and sensuous, sending a sudden quiver through her nerve-stream. 'It's not your help I object to, it's the fact that you seem to see help only in the form of money.'

'What other form is there?' she asked, puzzled.

'The only form that counts.' His words were measured. 'The kind of help that involves your time and your hands.'

Was he quite mad? Kelly wondered. She was aware that he was studying her, his eyes watchful as he registered the conflicting emotions which flickered across her face. 'You don't expect me to fill in for George?' she asked at last. 'I couldn't do a man's work.'

'But you could do a woman's,' he said very softly. And then, as she continued to look at him speechlessly: 'You could do Mary's work.'

She stepped abruptly away from him. More than ever she was aware of the claustrophobic atmosphere of the room—odd that she had not been aware of it when she had played cards here with her friends. But perhaps the atmosphere had less to do with the size of the room than with the sense of maleness now pervading it, a maleness that was so potent as to be dizzying.

'Let me go,' she ordered low-toned, knowing that her only way out of the room was past the lean muscled body which stood between her and the door.

'When you've agreed to my proposition.'

She sent him a burning look. 'I've never heard anything more absurd in my life!'

'Absurd?' He was baiting her, she thought, and taking pleasure in it.

'Of course. I know nothing about hotel management.'

He looked at her steadily. 'You could learn.'

He means it, she thought. He actually means it. This is not just a game.

Aloud, she said, 'I suppose I could. But there'd be no point in it.'

'There would. George will be operated on tomorrow. If you took over Mary's duties she could be at his side.'

If it was anyone other than Nicholas Van Mijden who was speaking these words, Kelly thought, she would understand. She would even be prepared to consider the proposition. She had noticed the love that existed between the Andersons, and she realised that it would make all the difference to George to have Mary by his side. She did not know what Mary's duties entailed, but it was probable that she could learn them. But the man *was* Nicholas, and an irrational rebelliousness would not let her give in to him.

'Mary wouldn't ask it of me,' she protested, thinking of the sweet-natured young woman with the pretty smile. 'She doesn't even know I'm here.'

'It's the very last thing she would expect from the rich Kelly Stanwick,' Nicholas agreed equably. He paused, a lazy smile lifting the corners of his lips, a smile which did not reach the dark eyes. '*I* expect it.'

It was his arrogance which made her fight him. 'You can't force me.'

'You only think that because nobody has ever forced you to do a thing in your life.' His tone was quiet, and very dangerous.

'You're no exception,' she threw at him recklessly.

'You want me to prove it to you.'

It was a statement, not a question. Seeing the glitter in his eyes, Kelly braced herself for the next verbal attack. She was unprepared for the hands that reached for her shoulders, jerking her roughly against the hard wall of his body. She saw his head descend, and tried to twist away from him, but he was quicker than she was. Easily his lips found hers, crushing them without mercy. His hands left her shoulders and moved to her back and down to her hips with a possession to which he had no right. Flames shot through her nerve-stream, fierce and wild, stirring her blood and dizzying her senses. Her body knew an irrational desire to respond, but her mind remained sane. It was with an effort of will that she kept her hands at her side and her lips tightly closed.

She was quivering when he put her from him. As he looked down she saw in the grey eyes an expression which she could not define. 'A prim virgin on top of everything else,' he commented.

Again his words had the power to hurt. Colour washed her cheeks, but Kelly kept her head high. 'I prefer to choose who will make love to me,' she countered icily.

'Gary Sloan will be getting no more than he deserves.' If she had hoped to put him in his place, the cool derision of his expression revealed that she had not succeeded. 'But perhaps that won't bother him. There'll be other compensations.'

Her hand was lifting to strike him when the door opened and Mary Anderson came into the room. Her pretty face was drawn and preoccupied, and her expression revealed that she was unaware of the tension in the room.

'Nicholas, I was wondering where you ...' Registering Kelly's presence in the room, she stopped. 'Why, Miss Stanwick, I thought you'd left.'

'I had.' Kelly marvelled that she could smile, that her voice was so calm. She refused to glance at Nicholas, for if she did her composure would crumble. 'How is your husband, Mrs Anderson?'

'Fortunately he's been sedated, so he doesn't feel much pain. They want to operate tomorrow.' Mary paused to dash away a tear. 'They're still doing tests.'

The grief in the woman's face caught at Kelly's heart, and impulsively she took Mary's hand. 'I'm so sorry it happened.'

'It was an accident.' If George's wife blamed Kelly for her husband's injuries, there was nothing in her tone to suggest it. She addressed herself to Nicholas Van Mijden. 'I'm afraid I'm going to have to ask for more help, Nick.' And then, turning to Kelly in explanation, 'Mr Van Mijden has given up hours of his time on his farm to help out here.'

Before Kelly could recover from her surprise, the rugged-featured man, who just moments ago had stirred her senses with the roughness of his caresses, said evenly, 'And now you'll have one more person to help you, Mary.'

'I don't understand ...'

'Miss Stanwick came back here for the purpose.' The look he shot at Kelly was meant for her alone. There was irony in it, coupled with warning. 'You'll be able to stay with George with an easy mind.'

'You mean...?' The question came on an incredulous breath of wonder as Mary Anderson looked from Nicholas to Kelly.

Miss Stanwick will take over your responsibilities.' Another glance at Kelly. 'I *am* right, Miss Stanwick?'

Formality was out of place from the man who had shown her just how low his opinion of her really was. Kelly would have liked to take his words and ram them back down his throat. She stared at him a moment before answering, and as she took in the steel in the long jaw and the enigmatic gleam in the narrowed eyes, she felt a momentary quiver. In a second she had herself under control. No matter what her feelings were for Nicholas Van Mijden——and by golly, she would see to it that she let him know exactly what she thought of him——for the moment there was a façade to preserve. It was obvious that Mary, who was watching her with an expression compounded of anxiety and hope, must be considered. Kelly owed Nicholas nothing, but Mary Anderson was another matter altogether. For Kelly had offered her husband money—a bribe, Nicholas had called it—to perform a mission which had endangered his life. Apart from her debt, Kelly realised that she wanted to help this woman, not much older than herself, with the wan face and swollen body and a heartache which no stranger could fully comprehend.

'Yes.' Kelly refused to look back at Nicholas. She forced a smile. 'I really do want to help.'

Only then, very briefly, did she glance aside. There was a gleam in the eyes of the man who disturbed her more every moment: an expression she had not seen before. Unaccountably her pulses quickened.

'That's ... that's just.... I don't know what to say.' Tears stood in Mary's eyes, moving Kelly deeply, and increasing her feeling of guilt at the same time. 'Yesterday I thought you ... But I was wrong ... Nicholas, I don't know what to say ...'

'I think Miss Stanwick understands.' With a gentleness Kelly had not suspected in him, he interrupted the incoherent flow. 'Perhaps before I drive you into town you could just fill her in briefly on the things you do.'

'Come down to the cottage with me,' Mary invited. 'We can talk while I change and put a few things in a suitcase.'

The hotel comprised a main building in which were the office, the lounge and dining-room and the kitchen, as well as the card-room. Behind it, and on both sides, were the guest cottages. They were round and thatched and whitewashed, many with creepers twisting up the roofs. The Andersons' cottage was a little distance away from the rest of the hotel, to give them some privacy, Kelly guessed. Bigger than the other cottages, it was also whitewashed, with bright flowering shrubs cascading over its walls.

While Mary was in the bedroom changing, Kelly remained in the living-room. It was small but with a look of cheerful brightness. Everywhere Kelly saw touches of Mary's personality—framed photos of her family, tweed cushions which she had chosen to match the curtains, and books on gardening and cake-decorating. It was easy to see that Mary was a person who loved her home and the things that went into making it. Small the cottage might be, but it echoed the friendly charm of the couple who lived in it, giving it an atmosphere uniquely its own. Kelly, whose parents' home was a villa big enough for ten people, felt a sudden pang of envy.

She went to the window and looked outside. The grounds of the hotel were beautiful. There were smooth landscaped lawns and beds of flowers, a cultivated loveliness against the granite backdrop of the mountains. In front of the cottage the Andersons had a small garden of their own. Here there had been no attempt at landscaping. Shrubs and flowers mixed and blended in a riot of colour and aromas, and beneath an oak tree was a weathered bench where they could sit together, alone and away from their guests. Beyond the garden was the view into the mountains. The morning mist was all vanished and the high peaks were sharply etched against the sky. Kelly wondered how it must be to wake daily to such beauty.

'I never get tired of it.' Mary spoke from behind her.

'I don't think I could either.' Kelly turned, and saw that the other woman had changed into a fresh maternity dress. Her hair was brushed and she had put on some make-up, but through it all worry and grief were still stark in her eyes. 'Don't worry about things here,' she said impulsively.

'Thank you.' Mary smiled her gratitude. 'I shouldn't be gone more than two or three days. But what with you and Nicholas the place will be in good hands.'

'I'll try my best.' Kelly was moved by the woman's simple confidence. 'Will you tell me what I should be doing?'

They went into the bedroom, and Mary talked while she packed her suitcase.

'I didn't realise how much you and George do yourselves,' Kelly commented at length. Somehow she had taken it for granted that there would be staff who did most of the actual work at the hotel.

'We did have more help,' Mary acknowledged. She paused and looked up from her packing, her eyes clouded. 'We had a bad setback about a year ago. It was hard to keep our heads above water, so we had to find ways of cutting costs. As staff left we didn't replace them where we felt we could do the extra work ourselves.'

'And yet the hotel seems to be doing so well,' Kelly ventured. 'So many guests...'

'It's starting to come right. The last two months we've been virtually fully booked. But financially we still have some catching up to do.' She looked down at her swollen body. 'I won't be able to work much longer, and the baby will be another expense. Not that we mind.' A sudden glow lit her face. 'We've wanted a family for so long. But I must be boring you.'

'Not at all.' At last Kelly was able to understand fully what she had done. She had held out temptation to a man who, against his better judgment, could not resist it. The money she had offered him would have gone some way towards buying necessities which he might otherwise not have been able to afford. But in tempting him she had also endangered his life. For the first time she understood the full reason for Nicholas's contempt.

'I'm so sorry that this happened,' she said.

'Don't be.' Mary knew instinctively to what she referred. 'George could have refused the money. We would have managed. He just saw it as making things that much easier.' She smiled, and Kelly had a glimpse of the girl she had been before worry and pregnancy had left their mark. 'I'm not angry. I'm just so grateful that you've come.'

'Mary, where does Mr Van Mijden fit into the picture?'

'Nicholas has been our friend almost from the beginning. He has a farm and a timber plantation a few miles south of here.' Her voice softened. 'He's one of the finest men I know.'

Fine? Kelly wondered what Mary's reaction would be at learning of the way Nicholas had demonstrated his mastery over her. 'I find him arrogant,' she said stiffly.

A hint of mischief appeared in Mary's eyes. 'Most women find Nicholas so sexy that they don't notice much else about him.'

Most women ... Nothing about the words justified the little knife of pain which slid between her ribs. In a voice that was so deliberately casual that it came out sounding flat, Kelly asked, 'He's not married, then?'

'Not yet. Though it won't be long now if Serena de Jager has her way. She's certainly the most glamorous of all the women who've chased him.'

Mary grimaced wryly as she closed the suitcase. 'Oh, Kelly, I almost forgot. You'll be sleeping here.'

'Here?' Kelly looked up, her eyes slightly dazed, her mind still trying to assimilate what Mary had said about a woman called Serena de Jager.

'Do you mind?' Mary saw her confusion, and mis-understood its cause. 'A convention is starting to-morrow. There's just one room left in the hotel and Nicholas will be using it.'

'Of course I don't mind.' Kelly glanced at the double bed. The bed which belonged to Mary and George; for her to sleep in it seemed somehow an invasion of privacy. 'It's just ... well, this is *your* bedroom.'

'It will have meaning for me only when George is well enough to share it with me again.' Mary straightened abruptly. 'Things should be fine, Kelly. But if you run into problems, or if you're uncertain of anything, you can always ask Nicholas.' There was the sound of a car outside the cottage. 'There he is now.'

'Say hello to George for me.' Kelly kept her voice light as Mary made for the door. 'We'll all be keeping our fingers crossed for his recovery.'

'I know that.' Tears glistened in Mary's eyes. She hugged Kelly swiftly. 'Bless you, Kelly, and thank you!'

CHAPTER THREE

NICHOLAS took Mary's case and put it in the trunk of the car. Then he held the door open for her and waited for her to get in. Watching, Kelly saw again the gentleness she had detected in his tone when he had spoken to Mary in the card-room. It was an unexpected quality in a man who was, on the surface, all toughness and aggression. It was a quality which made him human.

When the car had vanished from sight and Kelly was crossing the lawns, she wondered if the gentleness she had glimpsed was a quality which Nicholas reserved only for certain people—Mary, the wife of his best friend, whom he liked and respected, and Serena de Jager, the woman who seemed likely to become his wife. Presumably he loved her, and so he would be gentle with her too.

She felt an inexplicable pang of envy for something that she herself would never know, at least not from Nicholas. The tone of their relationship had been set two days before, when he had made his contempt clear without even resorting to speech. Today that contempt had been intensified. He saw her as a social butterfly, with more time and money than she knew what to do with. Even the fact that she had agreed to take Mary's place for a while would do nothing to alter his opinion—he knew that he had placed her in a position where she could

hardly have done otherwise. He would never believe that she herself had wanted to help Mary
once she had seen how much that help meant to
her. And Kelly would never tell him.

She walked a little faster. For the next two days
she would, of necessity, need to have certain contact with him. But the contact would be of a business nature only. She would waste no time thinking
ahead about Nicholas Van Mijden.

Yet as she approached the hotel she found it hard
not to think of him. The memory of the moments
she had spent in his arms was very vivid, shockingly
so. Her mind rebelled at the manner in which he
had treated her; at the fact that he had used his
superior physical strength to prove a point. The
man was not only arrogant, he was domineering
and tyrannical and altogether insufferable. She
resolved to make quite certain that he had no
chance to touch her again.

But even while she made the resolve, a voice deep
inside her, a treacherous voice which refused to be
stilled, told her that never before had she felt quite
so stirred as when the lean-fingered hands had moved
over her and hard lips had crushed down on hers.
Gary had kissed her often, and before him there
had been others. But never had she been kissed
with such ruthless expertise, and never before had
she felt quite so vitally and vibrantly alive.

She was frowning as she entered the main building and made for the office. She would *not* let herself dwell on Nicholas Van Mijden again. In any
event, she would be too busy with Mary's chores to
think of anything else. The two days would pass

quickly. Once she left Great Peaks Lodge she would never need to see the rugged-featured farmer again.

The desk clerk had obviously been briefed by Nicholas, for he did not look surprised when she asked to see the list of bookings. Already the first of the engineers had arrived for the convention which was to start the next day. The reservations had been made weeks ago, but Mary had asked Kelly to double-check to make sure that each man would have a room. The hotel would indeed be crowded for the next few days. As Mary had said, only one room was not accounted for, and that was obviously the one which Nicholas would use.

Handing the book back to the clerk, Kelly determined that she would do all she could to ensure the success of the convention. She knew enough about her father's business operations to know that a hotel which could be relied on would be used again. Conventions would be a good source of income, particularly in slack seasons. The Andersons must have been looking forward to this one. George's accident could probably not have occurred at a more inconvenient time.

Kelly attended to the duties on the list one by one. The day wore on, she wondered if Nicholas had returned from town. If he had, she had not seen him. She had managed very well without him. Perhaps she could even manage without him altogether. Mary's explanations had been fairly detailed, and if there was something she needed to know there would be a housemaid or one of the kitchen staff whom she could ask.

Afternoon tea was served on the wide verandah

with its lovely view into the mountains. A uniformed waiter brought out the tea trolley which was laden with cups and saucers. There was a dish of small home-baked biscuits, and a tall urn containing the tea. It was Mary's custom to preside at the trolley, handing out cups and saying a few friendly words to each guest. Now Kelly took her place.

There was an atmosphere of relaxed informality on the verandah. There were families who were spending their holidays at Great Peaks Lodge, and there were young couples, some of them obviously honeymooners. But the greatest proportion of guests was made up of the men who had arrived for the convention. They had been arriving in greater numbers during the last hour or two, and when they had been served their tea they sat down in groups, looking travel-weary and glad to be away from their offices for a while. Kelly guessed that to many of them a convention, despite the work it entailed, was also a welcome break from the daily routine.

'You're new here,' said one of the men as he took his cup from Kelly. 'I was expecting to see Mrs Anderson.'

Kelly looked up and smiled, liking what she saw. The man had evidently been a guest here many times before if he knew Mary's routine. 'Mrs Anderson is away for a few days.' She paused a moment, then, knowing that the incident would in any event be common knowledge before the day was over, she went on, 'Mr Anderson had an accident. He's in hospital.'

'I'm sorry to hear it.' The kindly face was concerned. 'Is it serious?'

'I ... I hope not.'

Something of her anxiety and unhappiness must have communicated itself to him. He studied her a moment without speaking. Then he said, 'Look, I'm all alone. When you've finished what you're doing, why don't you bring your cup and join me?'

They were the first friendly words she had heard since Mary had left with Nicholas. It was only now, as she looked into the pleasant face of the man before her, that she realised how much she dreaded Nicholas's return. She was also very tired. 'I'd like that,' she smiled.

His name was Andrew Lang, and he was in his mid-thirties, about the same age as Nicholas, Kelly realised. But there all similarity ended. Where Nicholas Van Mijden's rugged features gave an impression of toughness and steel and even a latent savageness, Andrew Lang appeared friendly and gentle and refined. Kelly did not need to know him better to realise there would be warmth in his personality, and kindness. Most important of all, she thought there would be understanding without judgment.

She had not intended to talk with any of the guests about what had happened. But with this man it seemed natural. After telling him of George's accident, she told him also of her own part in it.

'I'm so ashamed,' she said presently. It was an admission she could not have made to Nicholas.

'Ashamed?' Andrew Lang looked at her thoughtfully. 'I don't think you should be. We all make

mistakes, and you were thinking of your fiancé. . . .'
His expression altered a fraction, and she wondered
if he put the blame for what had happened on
Gary. Before she could say a word in her fiancé's de-
fence, he continued, 'What counts is that you're
making amends. And I think that's tremendous.'

'Really?' She looked at him gratefully. And then,
before she could stop herself, 'I wish Mr Van Mijden
was so understanding.'

'Does he know who you are?'

'Yes.' Looking across the table, Kelly met the
gaze of steady brown eyes. So Andrew Lang knew too
that she was Robert Stanwick's daughter. It surprised
her sometimes to realise that her father's name was
so well known.

'And that means nothing to him?'

Kelly pondered the question a moment before
answering. It seemed to indicate that her back-
ground *did* mean something to Andrew Lang. She
now wondered if it did to Gary, as it did to most
people with whom she came into contact. Only
Nicholas was unimpressed by her father's position.
It came to her with a sense of surprise that if his
attitude was autocratic it was also oddly refreshing.
She smiled wryly. 'It increases his contempt.'

'Mr Van Mijden must be a tyrant!' Andrew exclaimed angrily.

'So, Miss Stanwick, you complain about me to
our guests?' The question was drawled unexpectedly from behind her.

Kelly spun round, the colour draining from her
cheeks. Nicholas looked very tall, very stern. His

lips were curved in a smile, but there was flint in the narrowed grey eyes.

'How dare you!' Andrew Lang leaped to his feet before Kelly could speak. 'I take it you know who this lady is?'

'Doesn't everybody?' Nicholas laughed mirthlessly, then addressed himself to Kelly. 'Come, Miss Stanwick, you have work to do.'

In other circumstances Kelly would have answered him back. It was one thing to have agreed to stand in for Mary, quite another to be at the beck and call of Nicholas Van Mijden, to give in to him as if she were some servile creature without any spirit. A stinging retort was on the tip of her tongue, but she managed to suppress it. It did not need Nicholas's warning glance to tell her that too many interested guests were within earshot.

Andrew's hand was on her arm as she stood up. 'Have dinner with me tonight.'

'That will be impossible,' Nicholas declined for her. 'Miss Stanwick will be busy in the kitchen.'

Kelly looked quickly from one man to the other. Andrew Lang's pleasant face was taut with indignation. Nicholas was still smiling, but the sardonic glitter in the grey eyes was daunting. Tension sparked the air. For one uneasy moment Kelly wondered if Andrew was about to step out of character and do something foolish—like hitting out at Nicholas perhaps—something that afterwards he would bitterly regret.

'Maybe I'll see you later this evening,' she said in a hurried attempt to breach the tension of the moment.

It was only when they were walking towards the kitchen that she turned angrily on the tall figure beside her. 'You went out of your way to put Andrew in his place. Must you be so brutal always?'

'So it's Andrew, is it?' Nicholas ignored the question. 'I'll say this, you're a fast worker, Kelly Stanwick.'

'You make too much of a friendly chat over tea,' Kelly said icily. 'Besides, Gary trusts me.'

'How very misguided!' came the malicious rejoinder.

No point in continuing the sparring, Kelly decided. The man was insufferable, but perhaps the days would pass quickly. When she left the Drakensberg, Nicholas Van Mijden would be no more than an unpleasant memory.

To change the subject she asked, 'Any news of George?'

'I wondered when you'd ask.' His tone was level. 'The tests are not yet complete, but they hope to operate tomorrow.'

Caught by an inflection in the words, Kelly looked up quickly. Nicholas was watching her, his eyes narrowed and unreadable. She felt suddenly frightened. 'It isn't just his leg, then?'

'It's possible that his back was injured in the fall.'

'Oh, no!' Shock made Kelly numb. She stopped quite still and put a hand on Nicholas's arm. For a moment she forgot that the man was her enemy. 'Oh, no, Nicholas!' She did not notice that she had used his name for the first time. Even the fact that his arm had stiffened at her touch did not impinge on her awareness.

His eyes were as inscrutable as before as they skimmed the slender body from head to foot. But his voice, when he spoke, had lost just a little of its harshness. 'It was a bad fall.'

'Yes.' She bit her lip. Tears pricked at her eyelids but she tried to blink them back. 'He was lying so awkwardly and ... I suppose I should have guessed ... But ... Well, I was just so anxious that he might fall from the ledge that I didn't think about his back.' She dashed a treacherous tear from a soft cheek. 'Will he be all right, Mr Mijden?'

'I hope so,' he said gravely. Unexpectedly a hand reached for her chin, turning her face upwards. There were more tears now, trembling on her lashes, but he did not comment on them. 'You called me Nicholas.'

'Yes ...' The fingers on her chin caused a burning sensation, and in the eyes that gazed steadily down into hers was an enigmatic expression which was unnerving. She was suddenly breathless.

'Let's keep it that way, Kelly.'

Her heartbeat accelerated, then returned to normal when he added matter-of-factly, 'Informality is the custom at Great Peaks Lodge.'

As they went on walking Nicholas explained the nature of her kitchen duties. Most of it she already knew from Mary, some was new. She let him talk without interruption. She was only half listening to what he said. To her dismay she found that she was acutely aware of him, that his physical impact swept all else from her mind.

He was tall, even taller than she had at first realised, and he moved with a lithe, animal-like ease.

She glanced at him once, quickly, while he was talking, and then she looked away. There was something intensely disturbing about him, an air of sensual virility which made her feel uncertain and vulnerable, and at the same time very excited.

He had disturbed her from the moment she had first seen him on the fateful afternoon when Gary had asked George to be their guide. Every encounter with Nicholas had made her dislike him more, nevertheless she seemed unable to stop herself reacting to him. Just as the kisses in the cardroom had played havoc with her senses, so the hand on her chin and the use of her name just a few moments ago had been enough to quicken her heartbeat. With all the men she had ever known, and they included Gary, Kelly could not remember a similar reaction.

She was being fanciful, she told herself firmly. The novelty of her situation together with the arrogant personality of the man who had, in his own way, forced her into it, had combined to make her think and feel in a manner which was quite foreign to her.

She was glad when they came to the kitchens. Kelly, who had eaten in restaurants all her adult life, had never given much thought to what went on behind the scenes. The big kitchen was all shining chrome and sparkling countertops. It was still two hours until dinner, but already the place was a hub of activity.

One man was the meat chef, another was in charge of the vegetables. The menus had been prepared for the month, and the chefs and kitchen hands knew their duties. But with all the organisation, an overall supervision was nonetheless necessary. It seemed it was Mary's custom to remain in the kitchen not only for the hours before dinner was served, but also while the meal was in progress. Kelly would now take her place.

A little helplessly she looked about her. Even the lowest of the kitchen-hands must know more than she did. Then she saw Nicholas watching her, and it came to her that he was aware of her feelings, her sense of inadequacy.

She lifted her head. She *would* cope! Helpless she might feel, but she would not give Nicholas the satisfaction of knowing it.

'Do you think you can manage?' he asked.

'Of course.' She gave him an icy rejoinder with an autocratic stare to match his own.

'Good,' he said briefly, and turned away, but not before Kelly caught a glimmer in his eyes which, incredibly, seemed to indicate approval. Oddly it gave her spirits a strange lift.

The next two hours were among the busiest Kelly had ever spent. Not that she did any actual work—chefs, aides, waiters, all knew their functions. But, as if they needed a focal point, a frame of reference, they turned often to Kelly. No matter that she was not Mary, nor that she was totally inexperienced. She was Mary's substitute, and as such she seemed to give them reassurance.

Only when the dinner hour was nearing its end did Nicholas come for her. She followed him to a candlelit table in the corner of the dining-room. Until that moment she had not realised that she was hungry, but when the first course was placed before her she thought that food had never tasted so good.

For a while they ate in silence, then Nicholas said, 'You did all right.'

Kelly looked up from her plate. His eyes were on her, dark and hooded, for once with no suggestion of mockery. She wondered how long he had been watching her. You did all right ... Just four simple works, spoken quietly and without expression. Yet from the lips of this stern-featured man with the unrelenting manner they were praise indeed.

'Thanks.' For a girl accustomed to the suave compliments of dashing and debonair men, she was strangely breathless.

'Tired?'

She shot him a wary glance and wondered if he was about to launch into one of the verbal attacks she had come to expect from him. In the event, she was ready for him. 'Not at all.' She danced him a smile that was deliberately provocative. And then, as she knew that she had spoken no more than the truth, that she was in fact more exhilarated than she had been in a long while, the smile deepened quite naturally. She did not know that her eyes were wide and luminous in the candlelight, or that her cheeks were velvet and shadowed. She saw only the sudden tightening of his lips, and the little muscle that worked in the long line of his jaw.

Good,' he said curtly. 'Because there's even more to do tomorrow.'

Her smile faded. What a strange man he was! Just when she had imagined he was softening just a little, he became again the disapproving stranger.

His face was a chiselled mask of angular lines and his eyes were bleak. It was clear that the gentleness she had glimpsed in his dealings with Mary was something he would never allow her to experience for herself. An odd pain appeared in her chest, and with it her appetite vanished. Nicholas was still watching her, and she did not want him to see her distress. She dropped her eyes beneath long dark lashes, and played with food that tasted like cardboard all at once.

'Nicky darling!' A husky feminine voice brought Kelly's head swiftly up. A girl stood by their table. One hand rested on Nicholas's shoulder in a touch that was both possessive and intimate. But though it was Nicholas she addressed, her eyes were on Kelly. 'Forgotten our date, darling?' Well-manicured fingers stroked the fabric of his jacket.

'We'll have a drink together after dinner.' His tone was matter-of-fact, yet friendly. 'I've been rather busy, Serena.'

'Poor darling. Don't I know!' Another glance at Kelly. 'As if you don't have enough to do at the plantation. Now with this accident of George's you really are overworked.'

'George would do the same for me.' Was there a hint of impatience in Nicholas's voice? 'Sit down, Serena. You're just in time for dessert.'

Serena pushed a chair a little closer to Nicholas and sat down gracefully. Her hair was very dark and coiled in a chignon which revealed high-boned cheeks and finely-sculptured features. Her eyes were big and dark, and her lips were full. The clinging silk jersey dress revealed a figure that was voluptuously curved in all the right places. She was beautiful, Kelly thought, and understood why Serena de Jager had an advantage over the many other women who evidently thought Nicholas van Mijden attractive. Yet the other woman's beauty was one which she herself did not find appealing, perhaps because the eyes had a coldness and the lips, when they were not smiling, had a sulky pout. Involuntarily she wondered whether her dislike owed something to the fact that Serena had a claim on Nicholas, that from the endearments she used it was apparent that their marriage was just a matter of time. No! Angrily she dismissed the thought. For that would indicate jealousy on her part, and the idea of being in any way jealous of a man she detested was absurd in the extreme.

'Pear Hélène? Serena was eyeing Kelly's plate with a shudder. 'Not for me, Nicholas darling. You know I put my figure before junk-food.' She put a hand on one of his. 'Tell me about George, darling.'

'There's not much to tell. They hope to operate tomorrow.'

'Well, I hope he gets over the operation quickly. You can't run the farm and the plantation as well as Great Peaks Lodge.'

Kelly drew a swift breath of surprise at Serena's callousness. She wondered if Nicholas's reaction to the remark was similar to her own. When she glanced at him she saw his eyes were hooded and unreadable. Then her attention was jerked back to Serena as that girl said deliberately, 'In this case the inconvenience is so unnecessary. There was no reason for George to get hurt, was there?'

So they had discussed her together! Serena's implication could not have been clearer if she had put it into actual words. You, Kelly Stanwick, were the cause of George's accident. It did not matter that the implication was no more than the truth. In private Kelly still agonised over the part she had played in what had happened. She knew that her action was one she would not forget.

But now a new emotion stirred inside her. If she could not pretend that she was indifferent to Nicholas's contempt, she could nonetheless understand it, and had resolved to endure it for as long as she had to. But the fact that he had criticised her to this beautiful girl with the cold eyes and the hostile voice was not to be borne.

Her instinct was to shove the plate away from her and leave the table. But that would give the other girl a satisfaction she did not deserve. Not for nothing had Kelly spent so much time at banquets and cocktail parties. As her father's emissary these were functions she had had to attend. She had rarely enjoyed them, but they had at least taught her how to present a surface veneer of politeness and composure.

Now she forced herself to smile at Serena, a dazzling smile of unconcern intended to show that the barb had not succeeded in meeting its mark. Ignoring the veiled accusation, Kelly said instead, 'The Pear Hélène is superb. You don't know what you're missing.'

The pouted lips parted incredulously. Serena understood that she had been put in her place. But as Kelly forced herself to finish her dessert, she felt

no satisfaction. Artifice was something she had re-
sorted to so easily only because she had seen it so
often. It was not a natural part of her personality.
Even the momentary lift at the corners of Nicholas's
lips did not raise her spirits. The exhilaration which
had been with her when she had sat down to dinner
had vanished. She felt sickened and a little drained.

She finished eating and waited for the waiter to
take her plate, then she stood up. 'Will you excuse
me?' she said politely. 'I too have a date.'

Andrew Lang was alone at a table on the verandah. He stood up smiling when he saw her approach.
'I was hoping you'd come,' he smiled.

He drew a chair for her, waited while she sat
down, and then took the chair beside her. His
natural good manners warmed her. Gary could be
attentive and charming when he chose to be.
Nicholas showed her only contempt. It seemed a
long time since any man, especially one as pleasant
as Andrew, had treated her like a woman.

A waiter took their orders: a sherry for Kelly, a
gin and tonic for Andrew. It was refreshing on the
verandah. During the day it had been hot, but now
it was just cool enough to be pleasant.

Talk and laughter filled the air. Children played
on the dark lawns, and on the verandah each table
was occupied. Kelly saw that the engineers who
had arrived earlier in the day were enjoying the
holiday atmosphere which was a respite before the
start of the convention.

'Your fiancé doesn't mind you being here alone?'
Andrew asked.

Kelly looked down at her ring. Strangely the question was more difficult to answer than it should be. 'I don't suppose he likes it,' she said slowly.

'But he doesn't object?'

Kelly caught a note in Andrew's tone which indicated more than casual interest. She chose not to answer the question directly. 'Gary didn't have much choice really,' she said lightly. 'I'd decided to come back to the hotel, and that's all there was to it.'

'Strong-minded female!'

Andrew's smile was friendly, but it was evident that he would not press her. She could easily have left the matter at that. Yet, strangely, she was driven to defend her fiancé. 'Gary couldn't have come with me. He had to be in Durban today.' She wondered if the excuse sounded as lame to Andrew as it did to her. She changed the subject. 'Tell me about yourself. About the convention.'

He was a civil engineer, he told her. He built roads and bridges. The convention at Great Peaks was one he had been looking forward to for some time, it would deal with innovations and improvements in his field. Almost in passing he mentioned that he had never married. Till now his career had taken him to the lonely places of the world, places where he had not felt it fair to take a wife. Now, however, he had a consulting position in Cape Town, and finally he felt the need to settle down.

He spoke casually, but his manner was clear. If Kelly was not engaged, or if she regarded the engagement as something which could be broken, he would be interested.

She did not take him up on it, and knew that

this did not offend him. He was nice, she thought,
very nice. It was a long time since she had felt quite
so relaxed with any man. With Gary there was
always excitement, laughter and fun. With Nicholas
there was tension. There was also the knowledge,
much as she tried not to think of it, that his touch
could provoke sensations that left her weak. With
Andrew there was a feeling of peace and serenity.

She felt a small pang of envy for the girl whom
Andrew would eventually marry; that girl would
have a life of harmonious happiness, a husband who
would love her and look after her.

She looked down at her ring and wondered how
she would behave now if she were not already engaged. Would she meet Andrew half-way? Would
she let him know that she was interested? She had
always thought that romantic love was an essential
part of marriage. Love was what bound her to Gary.
Now, as she looked at the sensitive face of the engineer, she realised that with a man like Andrew a
kind of love could grow on its own.

And then, quite unbidden, an image came into
her mind, a lean mocking face with stern rugged
features and dark intelligent eyes. For a moment
it was that image which took precedence over the
flesh-and-blood man sitting next to her. Dimly she
was aware that Andrew was speaking, but she did
not hear what he said. Only gradually did his
features come into focus once more. She smiled at
him, but inwardly she was shaking.

Not far away a laugh rang out, husky and amused,
and Kelly froze. She recognised that voice—Serena
de Jager.

They were sitting at a table for two not far away. Absorbed in her thoughts, Kelly had not seen them come on to the verandah. She wondered now how long they had been there. As before, Serena was sitting very close to Nicholas. She was talking, her features vivacious, her gestures animated. Nicholas was smiling as he listened. They were too far away for Kelly to hear what the other woman said, but it was evident that she was both amusing and witty. Once Nicholas laughed. They could have been quite alone on the verandah, so totally absorbed were they in each other. And for the third time that day Kelly felt the inexplicable twist of pain in her chest.

She had been enjoying sitting in the cool fragrant air with Andrew. Now, all at once, her body tautened and she was no longer relaxed. She wondered if Nicholas had seen her. She knew that even if he had, she had long since ceased to be a part of his conscious awareness. For him there was only Serena.

Determinedly Kelly turned her eyes back to Andrew. Their talk turned to other topics—books, music, painting. Kelly found that there was much they had in common. The conversation flowed easily, one observation giving rise, quite naturally, to the next. Normally she would have enjoyed herself. But the charm seemed to have gone from the evening, and try as she would she could not recapture it.

The verandah began to empty. If the mountain air was invigorating, it was also sleep-inducing. The guests began to go to their rooms. For some the next day would be spent walking. For others there would be the talk-filled hours of the convention. When Kelly said she was tired Andrew said he would turn in too. His cottage was in the circle at the back of the building. Her cottage was at the other end of the garden. He offered to walk with her, but smilingly she declined the offer.

They walked together to the edge of the verandah. At the bottom of the stone steps they paused to say goodnight. Unexpectedly Andrew leaned towards her and kissed her lightly on the lips. 'Sleep well, Kelly,' he said.

CHAPTER FOUR

KELLY did not go directly to the cottage. Though she had not wanted to sit any longer on the verandah, she was not as tired as she had said.

Slowly she walked through the garden, and gradually she felt herself relax. For the past half hour she had been smiling, a smile that might have seemed natural to Andrew who hardly knew her, but which was beginning to strain the muscles of her cheeks. At last she could allow her face to rest.

The tension began to drain from her body. It was cooler in the garden than it had been on the verandah, but she did not feel cold. The air was fragrant with the mingled scents of the shrubs—the muskiness of the jasmine, the spiciness of the aloes, the sweetness of the lovely frangipani. The mountains were tall dark shapes against the star-studded sky, and the air rang with the song of a million crickets.

How different all this was from last night! Then the mountains had crowded in on both sides, and the sky had been no more than a thin sliver between them. Last night too there had been tension, but a tension of a different kind. For on the ledge far below the cliff path George had lain unconscious, and there had been the constant fear that he would wake and fall before the rescue party found them.

And then the rescue party had come. It was almost twenty-four hours since Kelly had begun the walk down the mountain with Gary and Alex and Sheila, following the stretcher back to the hotel. Twenty-four hours. It seemed so very much longer. For so much had happened since them.

Beneath a tree was a bench, and Kelly sat down. During the day there would be a beautiful view from here, across the garden to the bubbling trout stream and the mountains beyond. Now she could see nothing of all this. But she had no desire to go to the cottage yet. In the bedroom which belonged to Mary and George she would feel an intruder, strange and alone. Here, in the cool fragrant air, with the sound of the stream and the crickets, she could relive all that had happened.

She thought of George, and of the accident. All her life her father's money had been a constant factor, something which Kelly had no need to think about often, but which was always there. It represented purchasing power. It was also a means of opening certain doors. Though she had never thought of it consciously until this moment, she realised now that money had been the Open Sesame to anything she had ever wanted—even people, for there had always been men who showered her with their attention, women who wanted her friendship for reasons of their own.

The accident had shocked her. For the first time Kelly understood that money, when it was used unwisely, could be dangerous. In offering George an amount far in excess of the usual guiding fees, she had lured him with a temptation which, in his desperate circumstances, he had not been able to resist. It did not matter that she had done it to help Gary. In a way that made it even worse. For she realised now that together they had risked a man's life merely because Gary wanted so badly to win a bet.

Though she might never come to Great Peaks again, Kelly knew that the days she had spent here would affect her for a long time to come. She had changed, for ever perhaps. Sadly she acknowledged to herself that her feelings for her fiancé—even while she still loved him—would never be the same again either. She would try not to speak of what had happened, for to do so would make him angry, but she realised now that coupled with all the qualities which made him lovable, Gary's nature contained elements that were less endearing. In the first flush of their romance she had been enchanted by his recklessness. For the first time she realised that it was also childish.

Was it irony that this day had provided her with some measure of a yardstick? She thought of Andrew Lang, mature and pleasant and sensible, not as handsome as Gary, and certainly not as much fun, but very attractive all the same, and with an air of dependability which would be a source of great comfort to the woman who would one day be his wife. It was a long time since Kelly had met a man to whom she felt quite so drawn as she did to Andrew.

And then there was Nicholas. Much as she tried, it was almost impossible to exclude him from her mind. His image had the most irritating way of intruding where it was not wanted ... Nicholas was all the things she most detested—arrogant, conceited, domineering. She guessed that he was self-sufficient and ruthless. But he was not childish. She smiled a little wryly as she wondered if Nicholas Van Mijden had ever been childish. Reckless and daring? Yes. There was a look in the grey eyes that suggested he could be daring indeed, that he was a man who would enjoy a risk and take it with flair. But the risk would be his own. It would be undertaken only when all the consequences had been weighed very thoroughly. And it would never be at another person's expense.

How she could know so much about the man she hated was something she did not understand, but know it she did, and the knowledge gave her a strange sense of elation. Just as the fact that she was making comparisons, in which Gary could only be shown to disadvantage, filled her with shame.

It grew chillier. It was also getting late. Reluctantly Kelly got to her feet. It was restful on the bench beneath the stars, but if she was going to put in a long day's work tomorrow it was time she went to bed. The stars shed just enough light for her to make out the path, but the bushes and trees were no more than dark silhouettes, mysterious and a little eerie.

Something touched her foot. It was soft and slippery. She let out an involuntary scream as a tiny creature ran further, rustling the grass.

'A frog.' The voice was low and amused.

Kelly spun round. Her heart was racing. She clapped a hand to her mouth to stifle another scream. 'How do you know?' she gasped, when she could speak, and wondered if he guessed that her shakiness was only partly due to the frog.

'I'm a farmer.'

She did not need to see his eyes to know that they would be alight with mockery. It was too dark even to make out the expression on his face, but strangely no light was necessary. She had known him only two days, and yet every rugged feaure of the starkly handsome face was etched upon her mind. It came to her quite involuntarily that the face of her fiancé had never assumed such clarity.

She took a step away from him. To break the silence she asked, 'Where's Miss de Jager?'

'She went home.'

'She lives near here?'

'On a farm next to my own.'

Neighbours! Serena de Jager would be a frequent visitor at Nicholas's farm. From the degree of familiarity she had displayed in the dining-room, it would seem that they saw each other often. Kelly wondered why the thought should disturb her so intensely.

'She said you had a date...'

'A movie in the village.' His voice was lazy. Kelly knew it was absurd even to imagine that Nicholas could guess at the effort it took to keep her voice level. Yet oddly, she had the idea that he did know. It was not the first time she had endowed him with a perception he could not possibly possess.

'You didn't go because it was late. She ... she seemed upset about that.' Kelly wondered what drove her to pursue the conversation. She would never see Serena de Jager again. After tomorrow she would not see Nicholas either. His social life did not concern her in the least.

'Serena upset? Not once she understood. It wasn't our first date.' Nicholas spoke easily. 'It won't be the last.'

Kelly winced at the words. The pain that she had felt once before came again, and it baffled her. There was no reason for it, none at all. She had not changed the opinion she had formed of Nicholas the first time she had seen him. His undisguised contempt had made her think him arrogant and unpleasant. Nothing he had said or done since then had altered her views. Besides, she was engaged to be married. It could only be the unusual day she had spent which gave rise to a pain she could not remember having experienced before. Nothing else would make any sense.

His voice came to her through the darkness. 'How did *your* date go?'

'Date?' For a moment Kelly was puzzled. 'Oh, you mean my drink with Andrew Lang? Good heavens, that wasn't a date!'

'No?' he drawled. 'Seems to me you'd arranged to meet after dinner. And since the man had made no effort to join his colleagues he was obviously waiting for you.'

'Why should it matter to you?' she threw at him.

'It doesn't,' came the crisp rejoinder. 'But I wonder what your fiancé would make of it?'

'Gary trusts me,' Kelly said icily. 'I told you that before.'

'So you did.' There was no missing the derision.

She bit her lip. 'Why do you hate us so much?'

'Hate?' He shrugged. 'I don't hate you, Kelly. I don't hate Gary either.'

'But you despise us.'

There was no softening in his tone as he made no effort to deny it. 'Let's just say that I have no time for a bunch of parasites.'

'That's how you see us?' she asked, when she had caught her breath.

'What would *you* think of a man who allows his rich fiancée to use her money to get him whatever he wants? Who thinks it a good idea that she spend some more to appease her conscience and his?' He paused. 'Or were you only trying to appease your own conscience?' His voice changed as she stiffened. 'Your silence speaks for itself.'

'I won't even try to defend Gary to you,' Kelly said bitterly. And then, because she could not seem to help herself, 'You really consider me a parasite?'

'What else? Have you ever done a decent day's work before today?'

She was silent. No point in telling this arrogant man of the volunteer work she did at the hospital four days each week, when she visited sick children and spent many hours reading to them and helping them with their school work. He would not believe her. And if he did, he would not care.

'Have you ever really known who your friends were?' The question was unexpected. It also held a depth of understanding which defied Kelly to brush it aside with an untruth.

'Sometimes,' she replied guardedly. 'I know that Gary wants me for myself.'

He would return with a sarcastic comment, she thought, and braced herself to meet it. When he remained silent, she asked curiously, 'And you, Nicholas, does it mean anything to you that I'm Robert Stanwick's daughter?'

'Not a thing,' came the indifferent answer. 'Disappointed?'

'No,' Kelly said simply. She did not tell him that she was filled with a strange kind of elation. For a moment it did not matter that he did not like her, that he made no secret of his contempt. After years of men who fawned on her, who danced to her every whim, it was a novelty to come up against a man who was so strong, so self-sufficient, that social subterfuge was beneath him.

She was acutely aware of him, standing so near her in the darkness. She knew already how it felt to be in his arms. But it seemed that he did not even need to touch her for her senses to react to him. There was something primitive and basic about him, a compelling maleness which was so intoxicating that it called forth an answering response from deep inside her, a response that was just as basic, and intensely female. A response which she had not even known existed.

He was so near to her that she could reach out and touch him if she wanted. And she knew that it was what she *did* want. The depth of her wanting frightened her. Kelly had always prided herself on her common sense, on the fact that she had both feet firmly on the ground, that she was in control of her emotions. She had thought she knew herself so well. It came as a distinct shock to find that she did not know herself at all, to know that if Nicholas were to reach for her in the darkness she might not have the strength to resist him.

'Goodnight,' she said, glad that she was able to keep her voice so matter-of-fact. Even Nicholas could not guess at the turmoil raging inside her. 'I'm off to bed.'

'As we're going the same way,' he said, falling in to step beside her, 'we may as well go there together.'

She stopped quite still. Her body was rigid with shock. The cottage lay in a different direction from the hotel and the other cottages. They could not be walking the same way. Unless ... But no! She had *not* misunderstood what Mary had said to her earlier that day.

'I don't think I understand.' Her voice was stiff.

'No?' The low chuckle rang out in the dark, close beside her—too close. The sound of it was so sensuous that it set Kelly's pulses racing. 'It's quite simple. We're both sleeping in the cottage.'

'No!' she cried urgently.

'Yes,' he said casually, but with unmistakable finality.

'But Mary said ... she said....'—it was hard to speak through the dryness in her throat—'you'd be sleeping in the hotel, and ...'

'I'm sure she did say that,' Nicholas agreed pleasantly.

Kelly stared at him incredulously. 'She—lied to me?'

'Nothing so dramatic.' There was a mocking crispness in his tone, as if he found her confusion amusing. 'I had in fact meant to sleep at the hotel.

But a couple arrived just before dinner. There was no spare room for them. I gave them mine.'

'They had a booking?' Kelly asked tautly.

'No.'

'You could have turned them away.'

'That would have been foolish,' Nicholas said smoothly. 'Great Peaks needs every penny it can get. Especially now.' He put his hand on her arm and propelled her forward. 'Come along, Kelly. It's getting late.'

She was silent as she shook her arm from his grip, wishing that his touch did not do such alarming things to her senses. She needed to think, and she could not do that when the blood was pounding in her head.

'I won't sleep with you,' she said at length.

'I don't remember suggesting it.' Again the mockery which she so hated. 'Though I don't deny the idea is tempting. You're a desirable female, as Andrew Lang no doubt wasted no time in telling you.'

'Andrew Lang is a gentleman,' she threw out burningly.

'Where sex is concerned?' Nicholas questioned idly. 'I wonder.'

'You're the most hateful man I ever met!' Her voice was low. 'You will *not* sleep with me, Nicholas.'

'Not "with", my dear Kelly,' he agreed equably, 'but alongside.'

She thought of the double bed, and shivered. She could not sleep with Nicholas in that bed. Even if he did not touch her, and she doubted if she could trust him on that score, there would be no sleep for her with the long virile body at her side.

'Please, Nicholas...' Her voice was eloquent with pleading. 'We can't ... I can't...' A little desperately she searched for a convincing argument. 'What would Gary think if he knew?'

'Your fiancé has shown very little interest up to this point. There's no reason why he should start now.'

'You take every chance to belittle him, yet he's worth ten of your kind, Nicholas Van Mijden.' Kelly wished that she sounded more positive. 'Anyway, this conversation is futile. It's solving nothing.'

'As far as I'm concerned there's nothing to solve.' There was no mockery in the vibrant voice now. No derision. Just a complete lack of concern.

'You know that I will under no circumstances spend the night in the cottage with you.'

'And every room at the hotel is occupied.' Nicholas paused. When he spoke again his words were deliberate. 'Since the idea of sharing a bed with me is so distasteful, why don't you ask Andrew Lang if he will let you in for the night?'

Kelly bit her lip. 'You know I can't do that,' she said unhappily.

'Why not? Since he's so pure your virtue would be protected.' And now the mockery was back, hard and biting. 'If you do have any virtue left to protect.'

They were at the cottage now. Kelly spun round, caught by the meaning in his tone. He was so close to her that she had to lean against the door, but even then she could feel his warmth reaching her through the thin fabric of her clothes. 'What the hell are you trying to say?'

'Only that the role of outraged virgin doesn't suit you.'

It was hard to breathe through the tightness in her chest, a tightness that owed less to the malice of his words than to a closeness which was more intoxicating than anything she had ever known. 'I am a virgin,' she managed.

'Keep that one for Andrew Lang. He might believe you.' Nicholas spoke with uncompromising coldness. 'You travelled with Gary, you shared a room with him. You're no virgin, Kelly Stanwick.'

'I shared a room with Sheila,' she whispered.

'You don't make a good liar,' he accused harshly. 'Open the door, Kelly.'

'No!'

'Very well.' Roughly his arm thrust past her, pushing her a little aside, so that he could reach the knob. At the same time his arm rested against her breast. The feel of it sent a tremor through Kelly's nerve-stream. For a moment she could not breathe, could not move.

Then the door was open. With unaccustomed politeness Nicholas waited for her to precede him into the cottage. Quite suddenly Kelly's mind cleared. With a show of outward docility and reluctance she walked slowly through the doorway, then she whirled around to close the door. She had moved very quickly, but Nicholas was even quicker. A foot was thrust through the opening, blocking the movement of the door. Still Kelly did not give up the struggle. With all her strength she pushed against the door. The struggle lasted no more than a moment, then a broad shoulder pushed the door easily back at her.

Very deliberately he closed the door. She stood quite still, watching him, her reactions numbed, her body stiff with fright. Too late she eyed the open bedroom. If she had acted more quickly she might have made it into the room and locked that door. But it was obvious that Nicholas had anticipated that route of escape, for the tough wall of his body had already moved to a point where she could not get past it.

He stepped closer to her. An unholy light gleamed in the dark eyes. The line of his jaw was long and rigid and with the hint of steel that seemed such an intrinsic part of the man. Above the formal shirt he had worn for dinner, his throat rose strong and bronzed. The cut of his expensive trousers was narrow, revealing long muscled legs. Transcending the cut and quality of his clothes was an aura of sensual virility, of power and strength and uncompromising ruthlessness.

Kelly opened her mouth to speak, but no words came. She was rendered totally speechless by the sheer primitiveness of the male figure towering so ominously above her. His eyes ravaged her face, taking in every detail of the wide green eyes, luminous and frightened, the trembling half-open lips, the little pulse beating too quickly at the base of the slender throat. Then, blatantly, insolently, they moved downwards, over the rapid rise and fall of her breasts occasioned by the unevenness of her breathing, and then further still to the gently rounded hips beneath the soft fabric of her dress.

'Please, Nicholas ...' she managed to whisper at last, in an unconscious repetition of her earlier unheeded pleading.

'Please, Nicholas,' he mocked her. 'Please what? Are you asking me to make love to you, to show you what you've been missing in your milksop of a fiancé?'

She was so frightened now that she could only shake her head violently. The blood was pounding in her temples, and her legs were so weak that she could hardly stand.

There was no softness in the grey eyes that came up once more to hers. No understanding, no compassion. There was no tenderness in the hands that pulled her towards him, in the lips that closed on hers.

Just when she needed her strength the most, her limbs were weaker than they had ever been. But she did not give up the struggle easily. Later she would remember that she had pummelled his chest hard with her fists, that she had tried to twist her head away from his, and that, failing in her efforts to do so, she had bitten him and had drawn blood.

But with the memory came the knowledge that the struggle did not last long. For as his hands moved over her, moulding her body to his, and as the pressure of his lips increased, forcing hers open, the kiss deepening so that it tasted and probed and explored, treacherous flames of delight seared her body, and the effort to oppose him became even more an effort to oppose herself.

Nicholas raised his head once. 'Stop fighting me.'

'Never!' The word wrenched out on a sob.

'You want this as much as I do,' he said roughly. 'Stop kidding yourself, Kelly.'

She tried to answer, but his lips were on hers again, and the lean-fingered hands were sliding over her back to her hips, her thighs. And then he was lifting her in his arms, and as easily as if she was a doll he carried her into the bedroom.

She could not speak as he put her down on the bed. She could only stare at him with the tears welling in her eyes. She tried to sit up, but he held her down easily with one hand, while with the other he took off his shirt. Just as easily he slipped the dress from her body. He seemed to take her protests as nothing more than token resistance as he turned her sideways and slid down a zipper with an expertise which spoke of much practice.

Not a word passed between them as he undressed both her and himself. Kelly shuddered as he lowered himself on to the bed and she felt the weight of his body on hers. Dimly she knew that she must get away from him, that she must find a way to save herself before it was too late. But it was becoming increasingly hard to think as waves of sensation cascaded through her. Even while the last vestiges of rational thought rebelled against Nicholas's behaviour, her femininity responded with elation to the maleness which seemed to envelop her, to the strong beat of the heart against her breasts, to the roughness of his cheeks and the tautness of the long thighs against her own soft ones.

Nothing she had ever experienced had prepared

her for the ecstasy which filled her senses and dulled her brain. A hand left her back and went to a breast, cupping its fullness, then the lips which had ravaged her face descended to her throat, and finally to the other breast. Quite involuntarily her arms went around his back, and her fingers knotted in his hair. She heard his swift intake of breath, and then he was lifting himself from her. She saw him unbuckle the belt of his trousers.

It was at that moment that sanity returned.

'Nicholas...' a sobbing gasp, 'I really am a virgin.'

His hand was still on his belt as he looked down at her. His breathing was ragged, but the eyes that studied hers were bleak and hard. If she was devastated by what had happened between them, there was nothing in his own expression to indicate that he felt anything at all.

'Nicholas...'

'I believe you.' His voice was harsh. 'Perhaps I'm a fool, but I believe you.'

'Then you won't ... won't...' She could not finish the sentence.

'Rape you?' A short laugh. 'I get my fun whenever I want it, Kelly. Raping virgins doesn't happen to be my scene.'

He stood up. She was still lying on the bed. Her hands were on her breasts now, covering them from his sight, irrationally oblivious of the fact that he had touched them, that his lips had tasted them, oblivious of everything except an unaccountable feeling of bereftness and disappointment. Insanity it might be, but more than anything else she wanted to feel his arms around her again.

'Goodnight, Kelly.'

'Will you go back to the hotel?' she managed to ask.

'There isn't a room—you know that. But it just so happens that I prefer to bed down on the couch in the living-room.'

She should have been relieved, but perversely she was not. For there was insult in his words, and his meaning could not have been clearer. He had found her wanting. She had not come up to the standards of the women he knew like Serena de Jager ... In his eyes Kelly was not a woman.

'Sleep well, Kelly,' he said as he turned to the door.

Sleep well? She wondered if she would sleep at all. Long after Nicholas had closed the door, she lay quite still, just as he had left her. She heard him moving about the living-room. He was whistling softly, the sound of a man without a care in the world.

At last all was still. Very quietly Kelly lifted herself from the bed, walked to the door on bare feet and opened it just a crack. The room was in darkness, and she could hear the sound of slow steady breathing. She closed the door again and went to the mirror.

The face she saw there was quite unlike the one Kelly Stanwick normally presented to the world. Auburn curls were tangled and untidy. Her cheeks were flushed, and in her green eyes was a look of searing wildness. On her lips was a spot of dry blood

—Nicholas's or her own? She remembered she had bitten him. Was it possible that he had retaliated? Gingerly she took a tissue and wiped away the blood. It was indeed Nicholas's. But she saw that her own lips were bruised.

Quietly, for she did not want to waken Nicholas, she took a shower and put on her nightie. Then she slid beneath the sheets of the double bed.

CHAPTER FIVE

For hours, it seemed, Kelly lay sleepless. The curtains were open and so were the windows, for there was a netting-screen to keep out the insects of the night. The fragrance of the tropical shrubs wafted in from the garden, and the sky was studded with stars.

She lay very still. Looking out into the darkness of the African night, she relived all that had happened. Her body was bruised from the struggle with Nicholas. Her emotions were battered.

The rational part of her mind was still outraged with the manner in which Nicholas had forced himself on to her. It was this rational part which told her that she hated him now more than ever before; that the sooner she could leave Great Peaks Lodge and never see Nicholas Van Mijden again, the better it would be.

But there was another part of her which spoke differently. Paradoxically, this part was filled with a strange kind of elation. For Kelly knew that in all her life she had never felt quite so vital and alive, quite so feminine. And with this realisation came another. Lying alone in the stillness of the night, she could admit to herself that Nicholas had stirred her to such an extent that she had been fighting herself even more than she had been fighting him. There had come a moment in his lovemaking when her barriers of resistance had crumbled. At that moment there had been only the wish to surrender, to be as close to him as a woman can be to a man. She wondered what would have happened if Nicholas had not given in to her plea.

If this knowledge filled her with elation—for she had never known she could be so stirred by a man —it filled her as well with despair. In the society in which she moved there were many women who took their fun where they could get it. Kelly was different. She had always associated sex with love, and love with marriage. And here was the reason for her confusion. She did not love Nicholas—she *could not* love him. She was in love with Gary. And yet there was no denying that Nicholas had raised her to heights she had never dreamed existed, and in doing so he had turned her world upside down.

What would he say if he knew how she felt? Would the grey eyes light with the mockery she so detested, and the mobile lips curve in a cruel smile? But he would never know, she vowed. As soon as Mary Anderson returned, Kelly would be free to go back to Durban. She would not see Nicholas again. And she could only pray that his image would eventually cease to haunt her.

It was a long time before she closed her eyes. Finally she fell into a deep and exhausted sleep. She was awoken quite suddenly. Behind her closed lids there was darkness, but from somewhere near her came the aromatic smell of freshly-brewed coffee.

A little dazed, she sat up and rubbed her eyes. Only half awake, she was not yet fully conscious of her surroundings. And then her eyes opened, and she saw that she was in the double bed of the Andersons. Standing next to the bed was Nicholas, and in his hand was a cup of coffee.

Hastily she clutched at the sheet and drew it up to her neck. She stared up at him wide-eyed, disconcerted by his sudden grin of amusement.

'Such modesty,' he mocked her. 'I've seen you in less, remember?'

'Only too well,' she ground out. 'And if you had any decency you'd let me forget it. What are you doing in here?'

'It's time to get up.'

'I'm tired,' she protested. 'Nicholas, it's still dark.'

'It's almost six o'clock,' he said matter-of-factly. 'Time you got to work.'

His arrogance brought out the rebel in her. 'Get out of here!' she ordered.

'Not before I see you get up.'

The quiet authority in his tone had a sobering effect. Staring at him, she saw that he was quite serious. All at once she felt uncertain.

'I'm tired,' she pleaded. 'Yesterday was a long day.'

'And today will be even longer.' He did not speak unkindly, but neither was there any sympathy in his manner. 'Drink your coffee, Kelly. You'll feel better afterwards.'

'No.' Much as she longed for the taste of strong hot coffee, she would not give in to him. He would see it only as another victory. 'I will not have your coffee, and I intend to sleep for at least another hour. Now will you kindly clear out of here!'

A sardonic light gleamed in his eyes and a lazy smile tilted the corners of his mouth as he studied her. He looked tall and sleek and excitingly dangerous. He must have risen some time before, for he was dressed and shaved, and his whole bearing seemed fresh and alert. A navy knitted shirt hugged the contours of the muscled chest, and matching trousers moulded the long thighs. There was a sudden tightness in Kelly's chest as memory flooded too vividly back, and she could feel again the chest and thighs against her own soft body.

'So,' he said very softly, 'you like things the hard way. I wonder if Mr Gary Sloane knows quite what he's letting himself in for.'

With one swift movement he had torn the sheet from her clutching hands. Then he had scooped her into his arms, as effortlessly as if she was a doll.

Through the gossamer thinness of her nightgown Kelly felt the burning hardness of his chest. One arm was beneath her knee, the other was tight around her back. The smell of maleness filled her nostrils, so overpowering that she felt dizzy. And in her veins surged a flaming tongue of desire which made her weak.

'Put me down!' she managed to say.

'Did you think I had something else in mind?' he enquired outrageously. 'Sorry to disappoint you, Kelly, but there's work to do, and you and I are going to do it.' Without ceremony he dumped her on the bathroom floor. 'Have a shower,' he ordered. His eyes flicked the transparency of the nightgown.

'And then put on something a little more suitable for work.'

'You take pleasure in humiliating me, don't you?' she ground out bitterly.

'Is that how you see it?' He grinned, and for a moment there was a flicker of warmth in the grey eyes. 'Perhaps it's just the first time in your life that you've been treated as if you're an ordinary mortal.'

Certainly the first time that she had met anyone quite so arrogant and conceited! Also, whispered a voice deep inside her, the first time she had met someone who was her match. For the men she had known until now, with the exception of Gary, were people she had secretly despised. Men who flirted and flattered because they saw in Kelly Stanwick a chance to marry the daughter of a millionaire tycoon. Men who did not want to make their way in life by way of their own strengths as her father had done. As Nicholas Van Mijden would no doubt do—if he had not done so already. The revelation was sharp and lightning-swift. Nicholas would not bend to any woman for her worldly possessions. Gary was like him in that sense, Kelly told herself. He had made it so clear that he did not want her money. And yet while she loved her fiancé for the laughter and vitality he had brought into her life, it came to her that she did not look up to him or respect him. The fact had never bothered her before. She wondered why it should do so now. Except perhaps that for the first time in her life she had met a man who forced her to respect him.

And with that thought, quite involuntarily, came

another. Had Nicholas ever been in love? Did the
woman exist who could pierce the armour of his
arrogant self-sufficiency? Serena de Jager perhaps?
Certainly the woman was beautiful, even if Kelly
found her appearance too cold to be appealing.
When Serena was married to Nicholas, would he
ever subject her to the cruelty and detachment
which he had meted out to Kelly? Or would he love
her and cherish her and be a source of strength to
which she could turn in times of distress?

For Nicholas possessed that strength. His un-
pleasantness did not blind Kelly to the fact that a
woman who was loved by him would live in a haven
of comfort and security. Serena de Jager would have
that haven. A pain throbbed in Kelly's temple. It
was a moment before she suspected the cause of
the pain, Aghast, she stared at herself in the mirror.
It was not possible that she could be jealous!

When she had showered, she dried herself with
a roughness that was unnecessary. It was almost as if
the physical action could rid her of an appalling
flash of self-knowledge. Nicholas Van Mijden meant
nothing to her, less than nothing.

Yet when she was dressed, she could not help
being glad that the leather belt of her pleated skirt
emphasised the trimness of a small waist, and that
the deep emerald of her blouse emphasised the
colour of her eyes.

Nicholas was waiting for her in the garden. Kelly
stood in the doorway for a long moment. He had not
seen her yet, for he stood with his back to the cottage, and from the tilt of his head it appeared that
he was looking over the stream into the mountains.

He stood very still, one hand hooked in the belt of his trousers, his legs slightly apart. Yet even now, when he was relaxed, his body held a sense of taut virility which seemed to be with him at all times. It came to Kelly that if she had never met anyone as arrogant as Nicholas Van Mijden, neither had she encountered a man who was quite as compellingly masculine.

As if he knew she was watching him, he turned and came towards her. His eyes subjected her to a slow scrutiny, missing no detail of her appearance; the feminine curves shown to their most appealing advantage in the well-cut skirt and blouse, the eyes that were wide and luminous with the turmoil of emotions that she could not control, the cheeks that were soft and a little flushed. His scrutiny was deliberate, and with a surge of resentment Kelly wondered if he was comparing her to his glamorous companion of the previous evening.

The unnerving autocratic stance provoked a sauciness which was alien to her. 'Well, do I pass inspection?'

'Certainly.' There was a flash of teeth, strong and very white against the deep tan of his face. 'You're an attractive female.'

'Do you think so?' The question shot out provocatively.

'If you want me to prove it to you again, we can try it later.'

Grey eyes glittered wickedly at the warmth that stained her cheeks. 'Take a sweater, Kelly. The early mornings are cold.'

As she walked beside Nicholas to the main building of the hotel she kept her eyes concealed beneath long dark lashes. Absurdly the small interchange had given a lift to her feelings. Why this should be so was something she did not care to analyse too deeply. It was enough that she was filled with an exhilaration which thrilled her even while it disturbed her. It was alarming how just a few words from this man, an inflection of the voice, a certain shading in the dark intelligent eyes, could affect her. But it was important that he should not know it, for if he did, his power over her would be complete.

The sun was just rising. The tops of the mountains were shrouded in mist, and the forested slopes were a mass of greyness. The grass was wet underfoot, and the air rang with bird-song.

Already, after just a few days in the Drakensberg, Kelly was beginning to understand how the character of the mountains altered throughout the day. The distant slopes could be grey and brooding, or purpled with mystery, or blue with the haze of distance. Always they were fascinating. The escarpment gave off a sense of completeness, of eternity, which could bring peace to a troubled mind, and relief to frenzied senses.

Kelly stole a quick sideways glance at the man striding by her side. How little she knew of him! Just that he had a farm nearby. But she had seen him look at the mountains, had sensed his oneness with his surroundings. It was evident that he loved the Drankensberg, that he could think of no other place which he would want to call home.

Already there was activity in the hotel. Kitchen

staff hurried about their chores. A waiter walked past with trays of early-morning coffee which he was taking to the cottages. Nicholas unlocked the door of the office and switched on the light. The desk-clerk began his shift at nine, he told Kelly. Until then she would be on duty. Guests would be checking out at any time now, some would even be leaving before breakfast. Briefly, matter-of-factly, he told her what she must do. Taking it for granted that she understood his instructions and would follow them, he left the office.

For a while Kelly was very busy. There was more to do than she had realised. Once, during a lull, she thought of Mary. Not for the first time she realised quite how hard the other woman worked. She was in the last stages of pregnancy, yet she filled the duties of a few people cheerfully and without complaint. More than ever Kelly understood the hardship George's accident had caused. She understood too that by filling in for Mary she was helping the other woman in a way that no gift of money could have done.

Just before nine o'clock the desk clerk arrived. Nicholas walked in behind him. He told Kelly that she could leave the office now and that she should join him for breakfast. Kelly put down her pen, and stood up. She realised that she was hungry.

She was about to leave the office when the telephone rang and the desk clerk, who answered it, called her back. 'It's for you, Miss Stanwick.'

'Kelly? What the hell is happening?' Gary's voice came through the line, loud and angry. 'I've been worried!'

'Gary!' Kelly was instantly remorseful. 'I should have phoned. . . . I'm sorry.'

'Why are you still in the Drakensberg?'

'It's a long story.' Kelly paused and looked meaningfully at Nicholas. He was leaning against the desk now, one long leg crossed elegantly before the other. At her glance an eyebrow lifted sardonically. It was evident that he was not going to leave her to talk in privacy.

'Kelly!' Gary called impatiently.

'I'm here. Gary, I'm helping out at the hotel.'

'What!' He was incredulous. 'I understood you'd be giving the Andersons some money.'

'Well, yes ... But Gary, Mary Anderson needed to be with George. He'd had to have an operation.'

'What the hell has that to do with you?'

'I'm taking her place here.'

'Now listen, Kelly.' Gary's voice was loud and clear, and from Nicholas's expression it was apparent that he could hear every word. 'You're making yourself a martyr.'

'We were to blame for what happened.' Her knuckles were white, and she was holding the receiver with unnecessary tightness. 'If it hadn't been for us, George wouldn't have had the accident.'

'Then it would have happened another time. He's running a hotel, isn't he? Listen, Kelly, you shouldn't have gone back in the first place. But this ... These people have a damn nerve expecting you to work for them.'

'They don't expect it.' Kelly's voice was very low, very controlled. She wondered if either Nicholas or Gary understood the effort it cost her to maintain an outward appearance of calm. 'Nevertheless it seemed the right thing to do.'

There was a short silence, then Gary demanded, 'When will Mary be back?'

'Some time today, I believe.'

'And then you'll come straight on to Durban?'

'Yes, of course.' She was horrified at the hollowness in her tone.

'I'm missing you, honey.' The anger had left Gary's voice suddenly to be replaced by the eager boyishness which had once seemed so appealing.

'I'm missing you too,' Kelly forced herself to say, and wondered if Nicholas knew quite how difficult he was making it for her to give the correct responses.

'Hurry back, honey. There's going to be one hell of a party on Saturday. You don't want to miss it.'

'I'll be there, 'Bye, Gary.' She put down the phone and saw that her hands were trembling. She stood very still for a long moment, her face turned away from Nicholas. Only when she felt she had control over herself did she turn. 'We can go now,' she said tonelessly, suppressing her anger in the presence of the desk clerk who might otherwise have made too much of the incident to the rest of the staff.

Only when they were alone did she turn on Nicholas. 'Did it occur to you that I might want to talk in private?'

'It occurred to me,' he said without expression.

'Then why didn't you do the honourable thing and leave me alone?'

'I found the conversation interesting,' came the outrageous reply.

Kelly looked at him in stunned disbelief. And then she realised that she should not be shocked. Nothing Nicholas had done until now had shown any consideration for her as a person. 'No doubt you enjoyed it,' she flung at him bitterly.

'Immensely.' The grey eyes gleamed with malice. 'It was most illuminating.'

Anyone else would have been apologetic or embarrassed, but not Nicholas. The wicked gleam in his eyes indicated a complete lack of remorse for the invasion of her privacy. She could do nothing to improve his manners, Kelly knew, but she could show her displeasure.

At the door of the dining-room she stopped. 'I don't think I'll have breakfast after all.'

'I think you will,' said Nicholas, very pleasantly

'No. I'll probably see you around a little later.'

'Really?'

Lulled by his pleasantness, Kelly was unprepared for the hand which went to her wrist, encircling it in a grip of iron.

'Nicholas...' Her head jerked round, and she stared up at him. Her skin tingled beneath the lean fingers, and she wondered if he could feel the pulse that raced at her wrist.

'Breakfast, Kelly.'

'I ... I'm really not very hungry.'

'You'll eat all the same.' It was a command, uncompromising and not meant to be flaunted. 'There's work to do, and you'll be tired out before the day is half over if you haven't had some food to sustain you.'

'Don't you understand?' she whispered. 'It makes

me ill just to think of eating with you.'

His eyes hardened, and she saw the tightening of his jaw. 'Keep the histrionics for your boy-friend. They don't impress me in the least. Come along, Kelly. The waiters want to get finished.'

'Do you always get your own way?' she asked bitterly, when she was seated opposite him.

The mobile lips curved mockingly. 'Often.'

'And do you use your caveman tactics on Serena de Jager?' She did not know what made her ask the question, but having asked it she was dismayed to find that the answer was important.

'Serena?' The lazy smile was intended to torment. 'I have no need to use tactics with Serena.'

'I suppose she jumps into bed with you at the mere beckoning of a finger.'

Later Kelly was to wonder why she said what she did. But for the moment there was only an irresistible impulse to press on with her questions. Dimly she knew that the answers would have the power to hurt.

The grin on Nicholas's face deepened. A satisfied glitter appeared in the dark eyes. 'You're jealous?' he drawled.

'Jealous?' She spat the word at him angrily. 'My God, you're not only the most horrible man I ever met, but also the most conceited!' She gave a short laugh, and was horrified to hear the tiny sob at the back of her throat. 'Serena can have you. I wouldn't want to sleep with you if you were the last man on earth!'

'No?' An enigmatic gaze played on her face. It lingered for a moment on eyes that were wide and green and sparkling with anger and defiance. Then it went to the cheeks that were flushed with emotion, to lips that parted to show small white teeth. 'Do you really know what you want, Kelly?' he drawled slowly.

For a moment green eyes met grey ones. Only a moment. Even now, confused and angry as she was, Kelly could not sustain the unnerving perceptiveness of that gaze. She dropped her eyes, and, taking up a knife, began to butter a slice of toast with quick jerky movements.

How dared Nicholas take every opportunity he could to humiliate her! How dared he make an insinuation that was surely the most outrageous she had ever heard. When she could trust her voice she said, 'Yes, I do know what I want. I want to leave Great Peaks Lodge and join my fiancé. And more than that, I want to be sure that I never see you again—ever.' Briefly she raised her eyes. 'I can't wait for Mary to get back.'

She braced herself for another sarcastic onslaught, but incredibly it did not come. Instead she heard him chuckle, that low unnerving sound which could send the blood racing through her veins with its sensuousness. Involuntarily a quiver shot through her. She hated this man who sat so calmly opposite her. It must be hatred she felt for him, for the only other emotion of comparable intensity was love, and she knew it could not be that.

Yet even while she hated Nicholas, she could not deny her awareness of him. Unbidden came the memory of last night's lovemaking, and the recollection of her own unexpected responses. Now, while she tried to bite into her toast with a semblance of composure, she wished that she could push from her consciousness the need to feel his arms around her once more.

He had asked her if she was jealous of Serena and she had denied it. Honesty with herself brought a flash of self-knowledge, and with it the realisation that she had not told the truth. Yet she had meant every word when she had said that she could not wait for Mary's return. For Kelly's own peace of mind that girl could not reach Great Peaks Lodge soon enough.

In a sense it was a relief when Nicholas began to tell her what she should do after breakfast. As he explained the allocation of fresh linen for rooms just vacated, his tone was impersonal. If only they could keep the relationship on a business level, Kelly thought, then perhaps she could get through the rest of the day until Mary's return and go back to Durban with some measure of her usual equanimity restored.

They had almost finished eating when the head waiter came to their table with a question. She had noticed that the waiter was quick and intelligent, ceaselessly alert to whatever happened in the dining-room. Now he wanted to know something pertaining to seating arrangements for an outdoor lunch planned for the convention. Normally, Kelly realised, he would have taken his problem either to George or to Mary. In their absence he spoke to Nicholas.

She listened quietly as the two men talked. She was not concerned with a lunch which would take place on a day when she would no longer be at the hotel. But she was interested in Nicholas's handling of the problem. All she knew of the man was that he was a farmer. His normal contact with Great Peaks Lodge was in the role of a friend. And yet he approached the problem with a quick insight and perception. Kelly could see from the waiter's expression that he was satisfied with the solution.

As she listened, Kelly saw a new side of the man revealed. With Kelly herself he was mocking, arrogant, outrageous; with Mary he had been unexpectedly gentle. Now she saw that he was decisive and clear-thinking, that he could give authority with a quiet ease and with the knowledge that he would be obeyed. Unaccountably it gave her an odd pleasure to see this different facet of his personality.

A little wryly Kelly wondered if it was only she herself who experienced his ruthlessness. Mary would not believe it of him. As for Serena, she would know Nicholas only as charming and handsome—and an expert lover. A small knife of pain twisted in her chest.

She pushed her chair from the table and stood up. 'I think I'll make a start on the linen,' she said abruptly as Nicholas momentarily turned his head. Without waiting to hear his reply she walked from the room.

CHAPTER SIX

FOR the next hour Kelly was very busy. She had often travelled with her parents, and had thus spent much time in hotels. Fresh linen, well-served meals, helpfulness where it was required, all these were comforts she had taken for granted. For the first time she grasped the work and organisation that went on behind the scenes, and her respect for Mary grew. Even when she was in an advanced stage of pregnancy Mary's routine was long and arduous.

By the time she had finished with the linen Kelly's back was stiff from the unaccustomed bending. It was close in the room, and she felt the need of fresh air, so she went outside. Nicholas was nowhere to be seen. He had made no mention of further duties, but she knew already that she would be needed in the kitchen to supervise lunch. Until then she could sit down and enjoy the view of the mountains.

The verandah was almost deserted at this time of the day. The engineers were closeted in the convention room, and the regular holidaymakers were out enjoying the mountain trails or sunbathing beside the pool. Gratefully Kelly sat down beneath a red and white striped umbrella, closed her eyes and took long breaths of the fragrant air.

She had been outside no more than twenty minutes when she heard the clamour of men's voices. The engineers had stopped for a break. Some walked a little way through the garden, but most settled themselves on the verandah and ordered drinks.

'Kelly.' She looked up to see Andrew Lang smiling down at her. 'May I join you?'

She smiled back, gesturing to a chair. 'I wish you would.'

He sat down. 'What will you have?' he asked, as he beckoned to a waiter.

'Something very cool.'

Brown eyes studied her appraisingly. 'That sounded heartfelt. Been working hard?'

'I've been pretty busy.'

'I looked for you when I went into the dining-room, about seven-thirty.'

'I was at the desk.' Kelly lifted her face to the sun, enjoying the warmth and the freshness after the time spent in the linen-room. 'I'd put in an hour by then.'

'Van Mijden is really extracting his pound of flesh.' Andrew's voice had hardened. 'It seems he takes pleasure in overworking you.'

'I'm just doing the jobs that Mary would be doing.' Even as she said it, Kelly wondered why she should be defending Nicholas.

'Perhaps. But I think Van Mijden gets pleasure out of bossing you.'

Caught by the inflection in his tone, Kelly looked at him. There was anger in the brown eyes, indignation in the set of the lips. Anger on her behalf, she realised, and was warmed by it.

Last night she had thought Andrew the nicest

man she had met in a long while, and today the
view was reinforced. There was a calmness in him
which contrasted vividly with Gary's constant excitement. It was the excitement, and the fun which
accompanied it, which had appealed to Kelly. For
Gary had come into her life at a time when her
mother was ill, and when Kelly had had to act as
hostess at innumerable business functions where
the men were all too preoccupied with their
careers to be concerned with anything else. They
had flattered her, yes, had showered her with attention, but she had been conscious always that they
saw her as an inviting stepping-stone on the ladder
to success.

Andrew was very different from Gary. Kelly realised that his air of calmness and steadiness was
appealing. She felt a pang of envy for the girl who
would one day be his wife. Not for a moment did
it occur to her that she could be that girl.

If Andrew was different from Gary, Kelly had
already noticed at their first meeting that he was
different from Nicholas. The two men were more
or less the same age, and both gave the impression of
being intelligent and alert and successful in their
fields.

But Andrew, gentle and refined, had nothing of
Nicholas's taut masculinity, his air of strength and
power and sensual virility. He had none of the
physical impact which Nicholas possessed in such
great measure. It came to Kelly that though she
liked Andrew very much, the dizzying tension
with which she reacted to Nicholas was totally
absent.

A little crossly she wondered why she had made the comparison. There was no sense in it, no fairness. Yet even while her mind insisted that Andrew was superior to Nicholas in all the ways that counted, a stubborn voice that was born of the senses told her that in a comparison it was Andrew who was the loser.

She was glad when the waiter came with the drinks. She did not like the drift her thoughts were taking. There could be no happiness in it. For even if she was attracted to Nicholas a fact which the analytical part of her mind vigorously rejected— there could be no future in such an attraction. She was already engaged to be married to another man. But overshadowing even that detail was the fact that Nicholas despised and disliked her so intensely that nothing she could do would change his views even if it was what she wanted.

And she did *not* want it, she told herself firmly.

She took a long sip of the lemonade, then she said, 'Tell me about some of the places where you've worked.'

He seemed pleased. 'You're really interested?'

'Oh yes.' Her eagerness was genuine. 'I've travelled too mainly with my parents. But the lonely places were not on our route.'

For a while he talked, telling her of life in Central Africa where he had worked for the greatest length of time. The region came alive in his telling, and Kelly was a fascinated audience. At length he paused, and when he spoke again his voice had changed. 'Is it some quirk of fate,' he observed, 'that when one meets the girl of one's dreams she's either married or engaged?'

Kelly caught her breath at the unexpectedness of the words. There was no mistaking the look in the steady brown eyes, the inflection in his tone. She met his gaze a moment without speaking, feeling warmed and a little moved. But she could not say so, not unless she wanted more complications in her life, and there were enough of those already.

'Fate *is* strange,' she managed, as gently as she could. And then, thinking to change the subject before awkwardness could set in between herself and this very nice man, she asked, 'Are you enjoying the convention?'

He hesitated just a moment before answering. When he said, 'Very much,' his expression was as pleasant before, but Kelly could hear the note of aloofness, and she was sorry.

'How long will it last?'

'About a week. There've been a lot of new developments in the field.'

'And do you always come here?' A little of the aloofness was vanishing and she was glad. Whatever Andrew's feelings he was too civilised a man to let a grudge show.

'This is the first time.' He turned his eyes to the mountains, blinking a little at the glare. 'It's very beautiful here, isn't it? It gives the affair a slight holiday feeling.' And then, turning back to her, 'Sorry that I let my disappointment show just now, Kelly. I know you are engaged. But will you go walking with me when I have a few hours?'

'I'd love that,' she said honestly. 'But I expect Mary back some time today, and then it's back to Durban for me.'

There was a sudden hardness in Andrew's eyes.

'Perhaps I have no right to say this, but I don't understand how your fiancé could let you come back here alone.'

'It's really quite simple.' Kelly spoke as steadily as she was able, for the call with Gary was still fresh enough in her mind to be painful. It occurred to her that she was being called on to defend him more and more.

'He had business in Durban.' Kelly saw the expression in Andrew's face. If anything, it had hardened. It was obvious that he knew she was not telling the truth, had in fact known it all along. A little shakily, she said. 'Please, Andrew, can't we leave it at that?'

He recognised her plea for understanding, and his expression softened. 'All right, then. I can't pretend to believe Gary Sloan deserves you, but I won't refer to him again.'

Impulsively she put a hand on his arm. 'You are nice, Andrew.'

She felt his arm stiffen beneath her hand, and immediately regretted the gesture. She was about to withdraw her hand when he took it, making the movement impossible without being rude.

'Nice?' There was an odd note in his tone. 'I think I would prefer any other adjective but that one. The word "nice" coming from you makes me sound a little fatherly.'

'That's not true,' Kelly protested, and even as she said it she had a mental picture of Nicholas Van Mijden, and knew that 'nice' was the one word she would never use to describe him.

'Prove it.' The grip on her hand tightened. 'I'll

give the convention a miss until after lunch. Let's go for that walk now.'

It did not occur to Kelly that any agreement on her part would be seen as encouragement. Though he did not hide the fact that he was attracted to her, Andrew knew that she was engaged. She really did like him very much, and the thought of a complete break from her chores was welcome, as was the thought of being out of Nicholas's domineering manner.

'I'd love to go for a walk,' she smiled.

'Forgetting your duties, Miss Stanwick?' drawled a familiar voice from behind.

Kelly spun round, cursing the swift colour that coursed through her cheeks as she withdrew her hand from Andrew's. Nicholas was looking down at her, his eyes glinting mockingly at her flushed embarrassment.

'I've finished my duties,' Kelly said jerkily.

'You have not.' His voice was smooth. 'You'll come with me now.'

'I'm going for a walk with Mr Lang.'

'I'm afraid not. Come, Kelly. You're running late as it is.'

There was a small explosion of anger beside her as Andrew Lang jumped to his feet. 'This is absurd!' he exclaimed. 'You've been hard on Miss Stanwick from the beginning.'

Nicholas was unperturbed. 'From the touching scene I witnessed a few moments ago I gather she's lost no time in eliciting your sympathy.'

'That's not true! She hasn't complained. Nevertheless I'm not blind to what's been happening.'

Andrew's pleasant face was white with anger. 'I gather you know who you're dealing with?'

'Of course.' Nicholas's voice was bland, soft and sleek and dangerous. 'I told you that before—Kelly Stanwick, the daughter of tycoon Robert Stanwick.' Contempt sparked in the grey eyes. 'In my book, Mr Lang, the idle pampered of this world don't merit more consideration than anyone else.'

Kelly glanced from one man to the other—Nicholas, cool and haughty and contemptuous, Andrew, white and tense, his hands clenched into fists. She was reminded of yesterday's scene when she had wondered whether Andrew would try to hit Nicholas.

Hastily she said, 'Mr Van Mijden is right. I do have duties.'

'Only in so far as Mr Van Mijden'—a taut glance at Nicholas—'sees fit to impose them.'

'I want to do them.' Kelly battled to keep the tension from her own voice. 'I promised Mary I would.'

'If that's what you want, Kelly,' he said at length.

'I do.' She threw him a smile. 'I'll see you before I leave, Andrew.'

Very slowly Andrew's hands unclenched. The anger was still in his face, but he was making a visible effort to regain his control. 'Of course,' he said, a little formally, and then glancing at the engineers returning from the garden, 'I see the others are going back inside.'

As he turned away he looked deliberately at Nicholas, and Kelly was glad to see that though he had given in to him there was no hint of servility in his expression. He looked back at Kelly. 'I'll say goodbye to you later—alone.'

'Did that petty display of arrogance make you feel superior?' she hissed at Nicholas when they were alone.

The gaze that flicked the small flushed face was disdainful. 'I don't need gimmicks to bolster my ego, Kelly.'

She stared at him, hating him, while knowing that what he said was true. Yet something drove her on. There was the need to pierce his armour, to find a way of hurting him. 'You can't take it that anyone with sensitivity should enjoy my company,' she accused. 'It doesn't fit in with your idea of the way you'd like to see me treated.'

'You flatter yourself if you think you know my thoughts,' he observed sarcastically. 'It didn't take you long to find a replacement for Gary Sloan, did it?'

'I told you yesterday that Andrew is not a replacement!' Kelly's voice was low and stiff.

He laughed mirthlessly. 'From the way you were holding hands it certainly seemed so. But then I shouldn't be surprised.'

She threw him a burning look. 'And what's that supposed to mean?'

'Only that your sort has to be flattered and fawned on at every moment.' He looked down at her, and the sudden flash of white teeth in the tanned face sent a quiver through her system. 'You don't like that, do you?'

'Because it's not true,' she ground out low-toned.

'No?' he drawled. 'Your play of outraged inno-
cence doesn't have me fooled, Kelly. You don't have
a single scruple in that infinitely desirable body of
yours.'

She bit back the almost instinctive retort. Whatever she could say at this moment would be considered provocation, and even after such short
acquaintance Kelly knew how Nicholas would react to that. They were quite alone beneath a narrow canopy of branches, and she had had ample
evidence of his methods. At the thought of his uncompromising lovemaking her green eyes, in which
the rawness of emotion was only too clear, hid
quickly beneath long dark lashes.

A shuddering breath shook her body as she
drew her mouth in a tight line. She was letting
Nicholas get to her in a way no man had done before. It was bad enough that she could no longer
control her feelings. To let him know it would be
disastrous.

'At least you no longer try to deny it?' The words
cut in on her thoughts.

She lifted her head. She had herself under control now. 'That I'm unscrupulous?' She shrugged
her shoulders in a gesture of unconcern. 'If I denied
it you wouldn't believe me anyway, so why bother?'

A gleam came and went in the grey eyes. Despite
her rigid attempt at composure Kelly felt the quick-
ening of her pulses, but she managed to remain
silent.

'I wonder if Andrew Lang understands you any
better than Gary Sloan did.' Long fingers reached
for her throat and began a slow stroking movement

from the jaw down to the hollow with its feverish pulse. There was no affection in the touch, only a tantalising sensuousness which tightened her chest. 'Beneath that cool exterior you're a complex and hot-blooded female.'

Despite herself, Kelly could not stop her eyes jerking to his face. The familiar mockery was there, and the derision, but with it there was something else, a quality which she could not define but which was infinitely disturbing. Was it possible that Nicholas knew the drift of her unspoken thoughts? No! Perceptive he might be, and insufferably arrogant. Psychic he was not. Nevertheless it seemed wise to remove herself from his presence with the utmost speed.

'You said I was running late,' she said stiffly. 'Suppose you tell me what I'm supposed to be doing next?'

Just when she thought the breath would stop in her lungs the fingers left her throat. 'Checking the bedrooms,' he said, and his voice was quite without expression.

'The bedrooms?' Her voice shook just a little, and she could not look at him. Even now, when he was no longer touching her, she could feel a tingling where his fingers had been. 'I understood that there are maids who do the beds.'

'Of course. But it's Mary's custom to check the rooms after they've been done.'

They were almost at the cottages now. The thought of being alone with Nicholas in a bedroom—no matter that it would be the impersonal room of a faceless guest—provoked an involuntary shiver. Kelly felt she could not endure another minute of an intimacy which was becoming unnervingly sensual.

'I can manage on my own,' she said coolly.

'I'm sure you can.' His voice was as cold as her own. 'But I'll go through one room with you, after that you'll know what to look for.'

'That's quite unnecessary. As the spoiled daughter of a rich tycoon'—she threw the words at him with a modicum of his own sarcasm—'I've been in enough hotel bedrooms to know how they should look.' And, as he still continued to walk with her, 'Besides, you must have enough chores of George's to keep you busy.'

He stood still and looked down at her. For once she could not drag her eyes away from his. Despite his impersonal expression there was once again the disturbing feeling that he understood her thoughts. Kelly braced herself for a cutting insistence, or at the very least a sarcastic remark, but it did not come.

'Very well,' Nicholas said quietly. 'But do the job properly. Any complaints from the guests and I'll hold you directly responsible.'

Kelly lifted her chin. 'There will be no complaints.'

Again there was the brief gleam which she did not quite understand, and which had the power to disturb her. But all he said was, 'Be in the kitchen at twelve sharp.'

Without waiting for an answer Nicholas strode away through the trees. Kelly stood for a moment and watched him. As before she was struck by the litheness and power of his movements. Arrogant and hateful he might be, but there was no denying that Nicholas Van Mijden was quite a man.

She was trembling as she went into the first cottage and cast an expert eye around the room. She was at the door when she caught sight of her face in the mirror. Her cheeks were flushed beneath a honey-coloured tan. On her forehead was a fine sheen of moisture, and her hair had escaped its neat style and was an untidy tumble of curls. But it was her eyes which caught her attention. They were very bright, sparkling with unaccustomed excitement. She was not so naïve that she did not know what had put that look there. But that reason she could not accept, never would.

It was unthinkable that Kelly Stanwick, the girl who could have any man she wanted, should find herself unendurably stirred by an uncouth man of the mountains who neither liked her nor made any secret of his disapproval. Nicholas Van Mijden's physical attraction would be hard for any woman to resist, Kelly acknowledged that now, but she was letting him get to her emotions in a way that was absurd. More than absurd, it was dangerous, for she could not let the memory of the man haunt her long after she had left the Drakensberg and was married to Gary.

She glanced at her watch. Just a few more hours and Mary would be back. Until then she would keep out of his way, and after that she would not think of him again. No matter if it was difficult at first, she surely had enough discipline to exclude him from her thoughts. After a day or two even discipline would no longer be necessary. Once she was with Gary, Nicholas and the time at Great Peaks Lodge would fade from her conscious mind.

She glanced at her watch. At most a few more hours until Mary returned. Until then she would try to keep out of Nicholas's way.

It took some time to inspect the cottages, and by the time she had finished it was time to go to the kitchens. It was the third meal she had supervised, and by now the staff seemed to accept her quite naturally.

Once some instinct caused her to turn her head. Nicholas was standing in the doorway. He was looking straight at her, his expression inscrutable. She did not need to see his eyes to know that they would be mocking. Her body tensed at the sight of him, and she wondered if he had come with the sole purpose of checking on her. She forced herself to meet the hard gaze for a full second, and then, very deliberately, she turned her back to speak to one of the chefs. When she looked round again Nicholas had gone.

She managed to avoid having lunch with him. Instead of going to the dining-room, Kelly asked one of the waiters to bring a tray to the cottage. And let Nicholas make of that what he wanted! she thought defiantly.

When she had eaten she looked aimlessly around the living-room which belonged to the Andersons and wondered how she could pass the hours until Mary's return. In a while she would have to go to the verandah and preside over the tea. Until then, unless Nicholas came in search of her to unload further tasks, she had nothing to do. She could lie down on the bed and relax, but she felt oddly wound up.

Restlessly she looked out of the window. On a sudden impulse she walked back to the hotel, asked the desk clerk where she could find gardening gloves and clippers, and made her way to the rose garden beside the swimming-pool. She had noticed that the bushes were in need of attention—perhaps the Andersons had had to save on gardening staff—and since the cultivation of roses was her mother's hobby, Kelly knew enough about cutting and pruning and trimming to get by.

The midday sun was very hot. Now and then Kelly paused to rest a few moments. The mist had vanished from the mountains and the granite peaks were sharply etched against the metallic blue of the cloudless African sky.

It was quiet in the garden. The engineers were in the convention room, and the other hotel guests were either out on day-long walks or in their cottages resting. The air rang with the incessant drone of the bees which hovered over the ripe pollen of over-bloomed roses, and once two birds soared suddenly from a tree, their plumage exotic in the sunlight, loud cries emerging from slender throats as they soared skywards. A breeze came from the mountains, ruffling the roses and rippling the calm surface of the pool. Kelly, whose body was moist from the intense heat, revelled in the momentary coolness.

It was only when she was alone that she could fully enjoy the serenity of the mountains and the garden, and appreciate the sheer beauty of the setting. There was a sense of space and loneliness, a feeling of infinity and strength, which could not fail to make its impact on those who made their homes in the foothills and the valleys and the forests of the great escarpment.

Despite Mary's problems, and they were ones which Kelly in no way sought to minimise, she wondered if the loveliness all around her did not give the woman a strength which she might otherwise not have had in quite the same measure.

The Drakensberg was also Nicholas's home. Thoughtfully Kelly's eyes searched the furthest reaches of the valley. Somewhere not far away was a place which belonged to Nicholas. She did not even know what it was like; in the tension which crackled constantly between them, there had been no occasion for normal conversation. It occurred to her now that she might leave here and never know what he did. And while she had resolved not to think about him, she knew that there was a part of her which would always wonder about the things she had failed to ask.

The dull peal of a gong startled her from her reverie. Tea-time already! She had not realised it was quite so late. There was just enough time to go to the cottage to wash her hands and her face and run a comb through her hair, and then she would be expected on the verandah.

Many of the guests stopped for a friendly word as they took their cups. Yesterday she had been a stranger to them, but today they accepted her as part of the management. Kelly was aware of an odd

pleasure as she laughed at a small joke or answered
a question. Apart from Nicholas and Andrew Lang,
she doubted that anybody knew her name and thus
who she was. It was gratifying to be treated with an
unaffected friendliness that was meant purely for
her, and not for Robert Stanwick's daughter.

Andrew took his cup with a smile. She thought
he would ask her to join him when she was finished
at the table, but it seemed the tea-break had come
at an awkward moment in the convention and the
engineers had just paused for a few minutes before
going straight back to work.

'Mary's not back?' Andrew asked.

'No.' Kelly glanced at her watch, and frowned. If
the other woman did not come soon, it would be
difficult to leave Great Peaks Lodge before dark.

'You won't leave here without telling me?'

'Of course not,' she promised.

When all the guests had been served, Kelly
poured a cup for herself. She looked around her,
feeling a little lost. Andrew had gone back inside,
and though everyone had been friendly she was uncertain about joining one of the groups on the
verandah.

'Mary will be glad you did her roses,' drawled a
familiar voice at her shoulder.

It was odd how quickly her muscles could tense.
Kelly turned with deliberate slowness. 'I hope so,'
she said, and wished that she could keep the shakiness from her tone. She had been so certain she was
alone and unobserved during her stint in the garden.

'You've cleaned your arm, I suppose?'

She looked up cautiously. She could not guess the drift of the question, but she was ready for the sarcasm which seemed inevitable from her conversations with Nicholas.

'Don't tell me,' she said saucily. 'There's a spot of mud I forgot to clean off.'

'Not mud. You've scratched yourself.' For once there was no mockery in his tone. His eyes were hooded and impenetrable, making it hard to read his expression.

After a moment she shifted her gaze to her arm. There was indeed a scratch a little below her shoulder. It looked as if there had been some bleeding. It was the first time she had noticed it.

She made a small gesture. 'It's nothing.'

'Mary has some disinfectant. You'd best come with me to the cottage.'

A man like Nicholas worry about a tiny scratch? Kelly regarded him warily. What new trick was he up to? 'There's no need to fuss,' she said dismissively.

'Fuss?' His eyebrows rose, and he sounded impatient. 'Mary sprays her roses.' His eyes narrowed sardonically. 'Of course, if you'd rather chance blood-poisoning than trust yourself to my care, that's entirely up to you.'

'Your concern for me is touching.' She did not know what made her say it, except perhaps that the idea of being alone with him again made her so lightheaded that she had to say something.

He laughed shortly. 'My concern for you is only in as far as it would be inconvenient if your arm flared up and I had to take you to hospital.'

Kelly's fingers bit into the palms of clenched fists. Darn the man! He was more arrogant than anyone she had ever met.

'Save your concern,' she advised bitingly. 'Mary will be back long before anything like that can happen. After that I won't be your responsibility anyway.'

He did not answer, but his steady gaze was enigmatic. Disconcerted all at once, Kelly stammered, 'Mary *will* be back this afternoon, won't she?'

He shrugged. 'Come along, Kelly.'

The words were in the nature of a command, and Kelly had learned already that Nicholas was a man who assumed he would be obeyed. She was trembling as she walked with him through the garden in the direction of the cottage. She had been counting on Mary's return; it was not possible that she was not coming. Yet Nicholas's evasiveness had seemed to indicate just that.

CHAPTER SEVEN

SHE followed him into the cottage. Mary was methodical, and it seemed that Nicholas knew where to find what he needed.

When he had cleaned the area surrounding the scratch he opened the tube of disinfectant ointment. He began to stroke on the ointment, his fingers moving in slow movements that were so unbearably sensual that Kelly felt her pulses racing. She pressed her lips in a tight line to prevent them from trembling, and dropped her eyes so that he would not read her emotion. At his low chuckle, unnervingly near her ear, she shivered.

'It's that bad?' His voice was a husky tease.

She nodded. 'Yes.' Ostensibly they were talking of the scratch, but Kelly had the appalling feeling that Nicholas guessed at the true reason for her tension.

'You're a funny mixture, aren't you?' He studied her speculatively, taking in the wide green eyes that were frighteningly easy to read, the two spots of colour in the soft cheeks, the little pulse that throbbed at the base of her throat.

'Wh-what do you mean?' It was becoming harder and harder to speak through the tightness in her chest.

'All spoiled and sophisticated worldliness on the outside, yet a little naïve on the inside.'

He was so close to her that she could feel the warmth of his breath against her cheek. 'I don't know what you're trying to say,' Kelly countered jerkily. 'If you're talking about the work I've done.... I'm not Mary, but I've tried my best.'

'I'm not talking about Mary or your work, and you know it.' The low voice held a seductive throb. 'Though I don't deny that you've done a good job.'

'I never thought you'd say it.' His fingers were continuing in the same stroking movement, and she wondered, a little wildly, how much ointment Nicholas thought was necessary, also why he should see fit to rub the skin that was not torn by the thorns. 'Nicholas—do you think you could stop now?'

For a moment that seemed never-ending the movements of his fingers were, if anything, even more tantalising. Just when she thought she would stop breathing, the hand left her arm. She was relieved—and at the same time she felt stupidly bereft.

Without a word Nicholas stood up and walked through to the living-room. Kelly followed him.

'Nicholas ...' Her throat was dry. 'You didn't answer my question.' And as he turned to look at her, 'About Mary ... She *is* coming back this afternoon, isn't she?'

His eyes studied her. 'No.'

Kelly turned pale. 'That was the arrangement.'

'She can't make it. She'll be here tomorrow morning.'

'No!' Colour returned to Kelly's cheeks, as the

protest jerked from her lips. 'I won't stay here tonight.'

'You have little alternative.' His tone was without expression.

'Will you be here too?'

'My dear Kelly,' white teeth flashed wickedly
against the bronzed skin, 'what an unnecessary
question!'

She looked at him quite silently for a few moments before she spoke again. He was enjoying
this, she thought. He knew just how she felt—the
turmoil coupled with an almost pleasurable appre-
hension—and it gave him satisfaction.

'If the hotel is full you could sleep at your farm.'

'You know the answer to that one too.'

'You don't understand, Nicholas.' She said with a
note of quiet despair. 'I don't want to spend another
night in the same cottage with you.'

'I do understand,' he countered in measured
tones. 'And if you're honest with yourself, Kelly,
you'll admit that we both want the same thing.'

She stared at him wide-eyed. Her mouth opened,
but no words came. As a wave of desire swamped
her senses she could only shake her head in horrified disbelief. At last one word burst from her
parched throat. 'No!'

Then she was pushing past him, intent only on
getting out of the cottage, away from Nicholas, away
from a truth which she could under no circumstances accept. A strong hand seized her wrist, jerking her back from the door, and then he was pulling her roughly against the hardness of his body.

He had kissed her before, in punishment or to

prove a point, and each time she had been stirred against her will. This kiss was different. It was deliberately sensual, the expertise of the probing lips raising her to heights she had not dreamed of. Once, when he paused for breath, she managed to twist her head and utter a protest. She caught sight of his eyes, filled with an expression she had never seen before, not even in Gary, and she was frightened and wildly excited at one and the same time.

'Nicholas,' she pleaded, 'please ... let me go. ...'

'You want it, Kelly.' There was seductiveness in the husky throb of his voice.

And then his mouth was descending again, and his hands were on her body, moulding it between them, sliding from her shoulders to her back and then to her hips. She could feel the hard length of his body against hers and through her own desire she could feel that he wanted her. She did not know that she arched instinctively towards him, all rational thought gone now, filled only with the need to be closer to him, and closer. ...

At some stage he must have opened the buttons of her blouse, and now she felt his lips pressing against the hollow between her breasts. New flames were ignited, and involuntarily she shuddered.

It was only as he lifted her in his arms to carry her to the bed that she saw his face. It was the face of Nicholas Van Mijden, the man who could rouse her to an ecstasy she had never imagined possible, and who would despise her later for having been too susceptible. It was the face of her enemy, the man who had despised and ridiculed her since the moment he had set eyes on her. With the last vestiges of her resistance crumbling, and with every nerve and fibre of her body clamouring to be part of this man, reason came to her rescue.

This time when she protested, she did so with anger tinged with despair. For once she was quicker than he was. It was the despair which lent urgency to her movements, so that she managed to wrest herself from him before he could put her down.

It was only later that she realised that if Nicholas had really wanted her, the movement would not have succeeded. She knew too that if he had resumed his lovemaking, she might have surrendered completely and risked the consequences.

He made no move to stop her as she ran from the bedroom and out of the cottage. She was already outside when she remembered that her blouse was undone, her hair dishevelled. With fingers that shook she stood beneath the trees and did up her buttons and tucked her blouse into her skirt. Ideally she should have gone back inside to do her hair. But nothing would induce her to face Nicholas again so soon. Roughly she raked her fingers through her hair, and hoped she was in some measure successful.

Nicholas did not seek her out again that afternoon, and Mary's list mentioned nothing specific to be done at the hotel. If Andrew had been around Kelly might have suggested a walk, but except for the few moments at tea-time she had not seen him. She was in no state to go to the verandah and order herself something to drink. In any event she was far too restless to sit and gaze into the mountains.

Sitting would mean thinking, and her thoughts would inevitably turn to Nicholas.

Sooner or later she would have to think about him, and about the feelings he had awakened in her. But not now. Not until she had left Great Peaks Lodge. For she knew that the thoughts would be painful, that only the finality of a parting and the knowledge that there was no possibility of seeing Nicholas again could create some kind of peace out of turmoil. The fact that it would be a peace born of resignation, was something she would have to accept.

But she could not, would not, think about him now!

There was only one way not to think, and that was to keep busy. Even without Nicholas to delegate chores, it was not hard to find things to do. On the surface the hotel was neat and well kept. Although they could not afford as much staff as they needed, the Andersons had been clever at making the best of things and at preserving an outward image that was eminently pleasing. Yet now that Kelly was beginning to know the hotel more intimately, she recognised tasks that had been shelved to await a day when time and money were more plentiful. For one who was looking for work, it was not hard to find.

She was polishing a pair of copper vases which would look just right on the mantelpiece of the lounge when she glanced at her watch and saw that it was time to go to the kitchens. The sun was beginning to set behind the high peaks. Soon it would be dark. Despite what Nicholas had said, she had continued to hope that Mary would return. Now she knew that the hope had been futile.

For once Nicholas did not come to the kitchens and Kelly was glad. She did not want to face him. Later, when most of the guests had eaten and it was almost time for her own dinner, a waiter came to her with a message. Miss de Jager was dining with Mr Van Mijden and they would be glad if she would come through and join them. Kelly hesitated a few moments, searching for a believable excuse, before it came to her that no excuses were necessary. She sent a polite message back, declining the invitation.

Not that they would waste two minutes wondering at her refusal, she thought wryly. The invitation had been no more than a social politeness. They would be far happier without her. She did not have to be in the room to see them together—Serena, beautiful and vivacious, laughing at Nicholas across the flickering light of the candle. Nicholas, lean and tanned and devastatingly attractive, enjoying the company of the woman who would soon be his wife. Not for Serena his arrogance and contempt and derision. Those qualities were reserved only for Kelly.

Under no circumstances would she share a meal with them. Yet the thought of their candlelit intimacy brought a pain which was like a knife in her chest.

When she had had something to eat, Kelly found more work to keep her busy. It occurred to her that she could go to the verandah and look for Andrew, but the idea of spending the evening in the engineer's company, much as she liked him, was unappealing. There would be a façade to keep up, a constant air of bright unconcern, for not far away, Nicholas and Serena would be sharing a table of their own. Kelly was in no mood for façades.

It was almost ten o'clock when she lifted her head from a cabinet she was sorting. Her back was stiff and her head was throbbing—fatigue, she decided. She had been on the go since dawn, with almost no respite. That Nicholas could be the main cause of her discomfort was something she did not even want to consider.

Through the scent-filled darkness she walked to the cottage. A light burned at the door, but the living-room was empty. In the bedroom she took off her shoes and lay down on the bed. She was so tired that the effort to bath and brush her teeth and change into a nightgown was beyond her. In a while she would get ready for bed, but first she needed a few minutes of rest ...

The smell of coffee was aromatic, tantalising. Slowly Kelly opened her eyes. It was light. Vaguely she remembered lying down on her bed to rest. She must have fallen asleep and left the light on.

Quite suddenly instinct told her that she was not alone in the room. Green eyes opened warily. A tall figure stood beside the bed, bronzed and muscled and almost unbearably virile. In his hand was a mug with the steam rising from it, in his eyes a mocking amusement that sent the blood racing through her sleep-sluggish veins.

He did not speak, and for a long moment no words came from her own lips. In a rush the events of the evening flooded her mind, and she understood that she had slept the night through and that it was now morning. What was not yet clear was how she came to be beneath the blankets. She sat up, meaning to ask him the question, when she saw, to her horror, that she was clad in a pale-pink nightgown. It was the most diaphanous garment she possessed. With a little gasp she clutched the sheet to her chin.

'An unnecessary action in the circumstances.'

For one wild moment there had been the hope that she had in fact woken some time during the night, just long enough to get undressed and slip between the sheets. But the clipped statement, coupled with the wicked gleam in dark intelligent eyes, put pay to the notion.

'You couldn't have ... I mean, did you ...?' Kelly was stammering in her confusion. The fact that warmth was flooding her cheeks with colour did not add to her composure.

'Of course.'

'You shouldn't have,' she protested shakily.

His voice was dry. 'It was a pleasure.' And then, as colour burned even brighter in her cheeks, Nicholas said mockingly, 'If it's any consolation, it was by no means the first time I've seen a naked female.' He paused, and she saw the gleam lighting the dark eyes. 'Though not all possessed bodies which were quite as desirable as yours.'

'You find me desirable?' The words were out before she could stop them.

He laughed softly. 'Are you asking me to prove it to you again?'

Yes! The knowledge came that she wanted it more than she had ever wanted anything in her life. Her every nerve and fibre trembled with the desire to have him make love to her. It was a revelation which brought her no joy.

'No,' she said tautly, keeping her eyes down lest he read the expression which must be clear to anybody as perceptive as Nicholas. She curled her fingers in her palms, and willed her voice to emerge loud and firm. 'Get out of here, Nicholas. I can't help what happened last night. But I do want some privacy while I get dressed.'

Her heart did a double-leap as a hand cupped her chin, forcing her face upwards. Grey eyes looked down into green ones. There was no drawing away, no possibility for concealment, for there was something compelling about the dark eyes that brooked no defiance. Kelly's heart hammered against her ribs, and there was a hard lump in her throat, making it difficult to swallow. Later she was to wonder if she remembered to breathe.

After what seemed eternity but might well have been only seconds, the grip on her chin relaxed, and Kelly was able to draw away and look down again, but not before she saw the glimmer of what could only be satisfaction in the rugged-featured face.

He left her without a word and went out of the room. For a long time Kelly sat quite still. Even after she heard the outer door of the cottage close, she did not move. There was a buzzing in her head and her limbs were trembling. Above all there was a leaden feeling of disappointment. No matter that she fought Nicholas, that she seemed unable to exchange a dozen civil words with him, she could not deny to herself the knowledge that she had wanted —desperately wanted—to feel the hardness of his body against hers.

As she walked up to the hotel in the pre-dawn light she wondered when Mary would come. She could only hope that it would be early. She could not endure even one more day in the presence of Nicholas Van Mijden. Lifting her left hand, she looked at the diamond on her third finger. Such a short time since she had seen Gary, and already he was assuming an insubstantial quality in her mind. The engagement itself seemed almost unreal. It was with a pang of dismay that she realised how little she had thought of her fiancé in the time that she had been at Great Peaks Lodge. Not that that was cause for concern, she told herself firmly. It was understandable that she had thought only fleetingly of Gary, for with Nicholas's unnerving maleness ever-near there was little opportunity to think of anyone else.

This did not mean that Gary's importance in her life had diminished. Had she been disloyal to him? No ... Yes! The intensity of her longing for someone other than her fiancé could not be called anything else. When she reached Durban she and Gary would resume their relationship where they had left off. She would be as loving and considerate as she knew how, and hope that in this way she could atone for the manner in which her senses had betrayed him. She would never tell Gary of the emotional upheaval she had experienced at Great

Peaks Lodge. To do so would not only hurt him, it would jeopardise any chance of their future happiness together.

In thinking this way she was considering Gary. But what of herself? she wondered with a feeling close to despair. With herself she could afford to be honest. Would she ever forget Nicholas Van Mijden and the surge of emotions he had stirred within her? Would the madness that ran through her veins leave her when she was free to go? Or would she be haunted for all time by the memory of a tall man with rugged features and steady grey eyes, so that nobody else in her life would ever quite measure up to him? Come soon, Mary, she pleaded silently. Because if you don't there may be no hope for me.

Mary arrived after breakfast. She was pale and drawn, and though she smiled and was friendly it was clear that the time she had spent since leaving the hotel had been filled with anxiety. George had been more seriously injured than had first been thought, she told Kelly and Nicholas, as she sat with them at a table in a corner of the verandah. He had had one operation, and needed another, but he was weak and shocked, and the doctors wanted to wait a few days before proceeding.

'I can't thank you enough,' she said, changing the subject, and turning to Kelly, 'you don't know how much your being here has meant to me.'

'I couldn't make up for you,' Kelly said simply, 'but I tried my best.'

'You did more than that.' The pale face brightened in a warm smile. 'You've done a wonderful job, according to Nicholas.'

'N-Nicholas said that?' Kelly turned, and for the first time since the scene in the bedroom a few hours earlier, she looked directly at him. His mouth was curved in the slightest hint of a smile, and there was something in his eyes which was neither mockery nor amusement. It was the merest flicker of expression, one which would have meant nothing to Kelly had she seen it in anyone else. In Nicholas, however, the expression was enough to send her pulses racing and to fill her heart with an absurd happiness.

Through a blur she heard his voice. 'When you've had something to eat, I'll drive you back to town, Mary.'

'Back ...? Nick, I can't go back! I'm needed here.'

'You're needed at the hospital. You know you want to be with George.'

The blur receded as Kelly sat up straighter and listened hard to what was being said.

'I do want to be with George ...' Mary sounded uncertain. 'Oh, but that's impossible ...'

'Kelly has coped very well until now.' Kelly might have taken the words as a compliment if he had looked at her, even briefly, and if his tone had not been quite so casual. 'There's no reason why she can't carry on as before.'

If it was possible for Kelly's heart to beat even faster, then it did just that. She could not have moved, not have spoken. Fortunately she did not need to. The conversation was between Mary and

Nicholas, and neither one glanced in her direction.

'Now you *are* being absurd, Nick,' Mary reproached him. 'I appreciate what Kelly's done—she's been marvellous. But I can't impose on her any further.'

'I don't see why not.' A lazy drawl.

'Because ... Well, for one thing she must have plans of her own.'

'None that can't wait.' And before Kelly could draw breath at the outrageousness of the remark, Nicholas went on, 'And if you're going to tell me that the daughter of Robert Stanwick wouldn't work, that holds no water.' An undeserved hardness edged his voice. 'Besides, you'll recall that Kelly had something to do with the predicament you and George are in now.'

'That's only true up to a point.' Mary spoke firmly but without bitterness. 'George is an adult. He knew what he was doing. He could have refused.' She paused. 'Besides, Kelly has already done more than was necessary to make up for what happened.'

'I wish you'd look upon my help as an act of friendship.' Kelly spoke into the tiny silence that followed Mary's words.

The woman turned to her uncomprehendingly. 'You can't mean ...'

'I'll stay here as long as I'm needed.'

Later Kelly was to wonder which had come first, the words or the decision itself. She kept her eyes firmly on Mary, refusing to meet the hard gaze in the rugged-featured face not more than a yard away. If Nicholas felt that he had scored a victory, she would not give him the satisfaction of letting her see it.

'Your fiancé—won't mind?'

'Gary will understand.' For the first time Kelly looked at Nicholas, throwing him a glance of taunting defiance. There was an answering sparkle in the grey eyes which momentarily disconcerted her. Deliberately she turned back to Mary. Quietly she said, 'Your place is with George.'

'Oh, Kelly! You don't know...' There was a sob in Mary's voice as the words trailed away. Wide brown eyes shone with a dazed kind of happiness, and in the pale cheeks was a suggestion of returning colour.

A lump formed in Kelly's throat at sight of the other girl's emotion. Not until now had she fully understood the love which existed between Mary and her husband. It came to her in the same moment that this was a kind of love that she herself might never know. Her relationship with Gary was on another level altogether.

Against her will, and completely without thinking, her glance went to Nicholas. He was watching her. His expression was steady and watchful, and for once there was not a hint of the mockery she so hated. For no reason at all the lump in her throat hardened.

'I don't know what to say—except thank you. You've been wonderful, both of you.' A grateful smile embraced Kelly and Nicholas. And then, as a new thought struck Mary. 'Incidentally, when I was passing the desk Joe said every room was occupied. You shouldn't have given up your room, Nick.'

'I don't believe in turning customers away.' He responded on a casual note.

'But this way you have to drive up to Nicholas's farm every night.'

Kelly held her breath. So Mary did not know that they were sharing the cottage. Now was the time to tell her, to express her outrage and humiliation. Strangely the words did not come. Then she heard Nicholas say, just as casually as before, 'Don't think about it, Mary, you've enough to worry about as it is.'

Slowly, carefully, Kelly slanted him a look. The eyes that met hers held an enigmatic expression which she could not quite define. She lifted her chin in a token of defiance, but her heart was thudding against her ribs, and she was the first to break the gaze.

CHAPTER EIGHT

IT was a relief when Nicholas left with Mary. As Kelly busied herself with the tasks that were beginning to assume an aspect of routine, her mind was a chaotic whirl of conflicting thoughts.

She tried very hard to hold on to the expression which had warmed Mary's face when she realised that she could go back to George. But it was not easy, for intruding itself was a lean tanned face with eyes that were almost too perceptive. She *was* glad she could be of help to the Andersons, Kelly told herself as she pushed a tendril of hair from her forehead with a flustered hand. There was a depth of devotion between the couple which she had seldom seen before, and which moved her deeply.

But apart from the fact that she was being of use, Kelly acknowledged her own happiness at the chance to remain on at Great Peaks Lodge—a happiness which was quite absurd in the face of her earlier impatience to see Mary return. Even more absurd when she admitted to herself that it was a happiness which was concerned mainly with Nicholas.

Impossible to deny to herself that she was glad that the stay at Great Peaks Lodge had been extended. Each extra day here meant one more day spent with Nicholas. If this flash of honesty brought clarity to her thinking, it also brought pain. She was not so naïve as to be unaware that Nicholas affected her more than any man she had ever met, that he was constantly in her thoughts, that when he was nearby there was a feverishness in her body, a desire for his touch.

She was attracted to him, very deeply attracted. It was an attraction which stemmed from the physical appeal which the man possessed in such measure. Kelly looked up from the linen she was sorting and stared bleakly into the distance. There could be *nothing* but physical attraction in her feelings for Nicholas. Anything else would be unthinkable.

Quite apart from the fact that she was already engaged, Nicholas himself was not interested in her. He was evidently as good as engaged to Serena de Jager. Kelly had no illusions that she could hold a candle to that woman in appearance.

Serena de Jager ... At the thought of the woman the last of Kelly's unreasoning happiness faded. Had she been quite mad, she wondered despairingly, to let a momentary flash of elation propel her into a foolish decision, which had not taken into account the futility of continuing an association with Nicholas? Just as she knew that there could be no future with him, she knew too that every day spent in his company made the possibility of eventual heartbreak more inevitable. That she had strong feelings where Nicholas was concerned was a fact she could no longer deny. But the feeling was not love, she told herself fiercely. It was all a matter of chemistry, of an inexplicable physical pull which grew stronger every day. But even if chemistry was all there was to it, it did not alter the fact that the day would come when she might find herself comparing any man she met with Nicholas. She had done so already with Gary and with Andrew. Both had lost in the comparison, and through no fault of theirs, for it would be a unique man indeed who could match Nicholas Van Mijden, not only for arrogance and self-sufficiency, but also for the virile masculinity which he possessed in such measure. Kelly did not intend to spend the rest of her life making comparisons. She knew what she wanted—happiness with Gary, a contented marriage, children.

Today's decision, she sensed uneasily, had placed the happiness of her marriage in jeopardy.

A little wildly she looked around her. Through the open window of the linen room she could see the forests and the mountains. The mist had lifted from the peaks, and the granite edges were sharply defined against the blueness of the African sky. Normally the view with its impression of timelessness and tranquillity brought Kelly a sense of contentment and perspective. But for once the view failed to move her.

She was in a trap. It was a good half hour since Nicholas and Mary had left Great Peaks Lodge. There was no way she could call them back to tell them that she had reversed her decision. The trap was of her own making. She could have refused to stay on—Mary herself had admitted that George was out of danger—but she hadn't done so.

Leaving the window, Kelly went back to the table and began to fold the towels. She would avoid Nicholas. As much as she could, she would minimise all contact with him. If blind emotion had led her into a trap, conscious calculation would lessen the impact of its danger.

It was noon when Kelly saw a long white car streak up the drive of the hotel. Nicholas was back. There was a momentary tensing of muscles, then, quite deliberately, she forced herself to relax. She had made a decision and she would abide by it. She did not meet the car, and later when it was time to go to the kitchens she kept herself busy and refused to look towards the door where Nicholas could at any moment appear.

She wondered how she would avoid lunching with him. In the event it was simple. Nicholas was in a hurry, it seemed that he was needed at his farm. When Kelly sent word by one of the waiters that he should start without her, he did so. Through her relief at having achieved her objective, she was conscious of a disappointment which made her own meal, when she eventually sat down to it, lose its flavour.

Andrew was on the shaded verandah when she came out of the dining-room. He was alone, and she wondered if he had been expecting her. With a smile she sat down at his table. He was happy to hear that she was staying a while longer at Great Peaks, but surprised as well.

'Van Mijden forced your hand?' His tone was light enough, but she saw a perceptive understanding in the brown eyes.

'Nicholas?' Kelly laughed, and hoped he didn't hear the forced note. 'Goodness, no! George is far from well. In the circumstances, it's better for Mary to be with him.'

For a moment he did not answer. He knows, Kelly thought, he knows that Nicholas was behind this and that I found myself unable to refuse.

'I won't say I'm sorry.' Andrew's tone was measured. 'In fact I'm glad. Kelly, the convention ends tomorrow. I have some leave due to me, and I may spend it here.'

Her eyes had been on the mountains. At his words she turned, caught by something in his voice. He was watching her. There was warmth in his eyes, as well as a question.

'How do you feel about it, Kelly?'

It was a loaded question, and it should not have surprised her. Andrew had shown from the start that he liked her. But at this moment Kelly was in no mood for further complications. There was Gary, and an engagement which, despite all her efforts, she was beginning to regret. There was Nicholas, and the power of an attraction which threatened to overwhelm her. And now there was Andrew, a man she liked and respected, but whom she looked on purely as a friend. Please don't spoil our relationship, she pleaded silently. I so badly need a friend.

'Well, Kelly?' he persisted.

'I think it's an excellent idea,' she said steadily. 'You've been working hard. What better place than the mountains for a rest?'

Disappointment came and went in his expression, so quickly that if she had not been watching his reaction she might not have noticed it. In a moment Andrew had himself under control, but Kelly knew that she had hurt him, and she was sorry.

When Kelly had finished the lemonade Andrew had ordered for her she glanced at her watch and stood up. 'Time to get back to my duties, I'm afraid. Thanks for the drink, Andrew.'

'My pleasure.' His eyes were steady, betraying none of the hurt feelings she had glimpsed in them a few minutes earlier. She was about to walk from the table when a hand took hers. 'Watch it with Van Mijden.'

'What!' The breath jerked in her throat.

'He's a tough man, Kelly. And he's as good as engaged.'

She swallowed hard. 'I'm engaged too.' And then, wishing she could do something about the brittleness of her manner, she managed a smile. 'Thanks for the warning, Andrew, but there's really no need to worry about me.'

For the rest of the day she managed to stay out of Nicholas's way. She saw him now and then, a tall lean figure, bronzed and purposeful, standing out easily in the gardens or among the guests. But she was able to programme her movements so that she did not run into him. Once in the kitchen, before dinner, she became aware that she was being watched. She did not look up—she did not need to. Only one person could affect her so intensely; as if an invisible wave of feeling sparked the distance between them. A little later, when she could lift her eyes to the door without being observed, she saw that he had gone.

Dinner was a meal which she dreaded, but there was something she dreaded equally—the necessity of a phone-call to Gary. She remembered his initial reaction to the idea of her helping out at Great Peaks Lodge. The fact that she would now stay even longer than she had anticipated would make him very angry; he would feel that she had put the Andersons before himself. She was dialling the number when it came to her that she had made her decision without considering Gary's reaction. And then with a pang she realised that she had hardly given him a thought until this moment.

He was as angry as she had expected. 'What the hell is this?' His voice was strident through the wires.

'I'm helping out, Gary. . . .'

'You said that two days ago. What are you playing at, Kelly?'

'Gary. . .' She tried hard to keep her tone calm. 'Please understand.'

'No, Kelly, I don't understand. I don't intend to. This Good Samaritan act is totally out of character.' He paused a little. 'That fellow Van Mijden has something to do with this.'

'No!' She was shaken by his perceptiveness. 'I'm not influenced by Nicholas . . . Mr Van Mijden . . .'

'The hell you're not!' He exploded angrily.

Kelly drew a breath. Looking down, she saw that the hand that gripped the receiver was white. 'George Anderson needs further treatment.' Her voice was as steady as she could make it.

'You said he was out of danger.' There was an uninterested flatness in Gary's tone. It saddened Kelly that she could visualise a petulance about his mouth, a sulkiness in his eyes. She had never before given conscious thought to these aspects—childish aspects she had to acknowledge—of Gary's nature. Why did she need to think of them now? Gary's resentment was justified in the circumstances.

'He is out of danger,' she admitted. 'But Mary should be with him.'

'I don't agree.' There was no mistaking the petulance now.

'You'd want me with you if you were ill,' Kelly put it to him as gently as she could.

'Are you sure *you* want to be with *me*?' A new note had crept into his tone. 'Under any circumstances?'

The question was so unexpected that for a moment Kelly stopped breathing. It was only when her heartbeat had returned to its normal pace that she understood the strangeness of her reaction. It was not the idea of losing Gary which had caused her heart to race. Rather it was the thought of the implications which could follow the break—implications, she realised a moment later, which could have no meaning at all, for their relevance would be entirely one-sided.

'Well, Kelly, are you saying you want to end the engagement?'

There was a brittleness in his tone, reminding her that she had not answered the earlier question. 'Of course not,' she said, and was surprised that she could sound quite so normal. And then, on an impulse which startled her even as she spoke the words, 'But Gary, perhaps we should give ourselves a little more time to think . . .'

She heard the swift intake of breath at the other end of the line. 'Then you *do* want to end it.'

'I don't know...' She was trembling now. 'It's just ... we may have rushed into this. We ... well, we really don't know each other very well, Gary. And ...' a hint of despair in her voice, 'all I'm saying is that we should give ourselves a chance to think if we're doing the right thing.'

A hoarse expletive floated through the line. Then Gary said, 'Tell Nicholas Van Mijden to keep out of my way. I might just break his bloody neck for him if he doesn't!'

Kelly remained silent. Irrelevantly the thought came to her that in any fight it was Gary who would be in danger of being hurt.

When he spoke again her fiancé had regained some measure of composure and Kelly was glad. 'All right, then.' His voice was even. 'But we'll both do the thinking, Kelly.'

'That's what I meant.' It was time to end the conversation. After what had been said any small talk would have been absurd. 'I'll speak to you in a day or two, Gary.'

Even before the phone call, the idea of dinner with Nicholas had been disturbing. Now it was an ordeal which she could not got through with. There was more to it than the fact that the tall man with the stern features could send the adrenalin pumping through her veins, or that after her decision today she would find it even harder to meet the sardonic grey eyes. There was more to it than the fact that since the call with Gary she had lost her appetite.

In Kelly's mind she knew that the engagement was as good as ended. She knew too that her attitude stemmed only in part to a new insight into her fiancé's character. Apart from the growing knowledge that she and Gary might not be the ideal match she had once hoped, a new factor had entered the situation: Nicholas. It was one thing to tell herself, with a firmness that was having to become increasingly more deliberate, that she did not care for the man, that she actually disliked him. It was quite another to find herself contending with emotions and sensations she had never experienced before. If she did not love Nicholas Van Mijden—and everything considered that was surely impossible—it was hard to put another name to the very dynamic and positive feelings which he aroused in her.

Somehow she must find a way of coming to terms with the situation. If the forests seemed suddenly greener, the air sweeter, the sky bluer, there was also the new turmoil of indecision, the doubts, the fears. There was the knowledge that what she was beginning to desire more and more—useless to push the appalling truth from her mind—she could never attain.

She could not sit down to a meal with Nicholas. No matter what he might think of her behaviour, eating with him at the candlelit table in the corner of the dining-room was more than she could endure. If there was a valid excuse she could make, she was too overwrought to think of it. When she was finished in the kitchen she slipped out of the hotel without a word to anyone.

It was quiet in the garden. Away from the verandah, with its sounds of clinking glasses and
laughter and talk, there was only the shrilling of
the crickets and the occasional croak of a frog. A
crescent moon hung in the sky, silvering the trees
and the bushes, and revealing the blurred edges of
the mountains. The air was warm and sweet with
the mingled scents of the shrubs. As Kelly walked
through the garden she felt calmer than she had
been all day.

'Well, Kelly.' The words vibrated through the
darkness, startling her.

She jerked around. 'Nicholas! I ... I didn't hear
you ...'

'You'd have made yourself invisible if you had.'
There was the usual mockery in his tone, but with it
there was something else, a quality which Kelly
could not quite define.

Kelly licked dry lips. 'What do you mean?'

'You've been avoiding me all day.'

'I've been busy,' she hedged.

'You certainly have.' The sardonic inflection revealed that she had not fooled him. 'For a girl who's
supposed to be one of the idle rich you manage to
dredge up tasks Mary never thought of.'

'You wanted to show the idle rich what it was
like to work. That was the general idea, wasn't it?'
Kelly tossed at him saucily.

'You deny that you were avoiding me?' His voice
was soft, and all the more dangerous for it.

Kelly swallowed. He was standing very near her.
Even in the dark she could see the litheness of the
tall figure, could sense the aura of sensualness and

virility. It was hard to speak naturally.

'I was busy, Nicholas, and I guess I didn't happen to see you around. I'm sorry if you thought I was avoiding you on purpose.'

'Very prim. And not very convincing, my dear.' She could not see his eyes in the darkness, but his tone was suddenly rough. 'You don't only play games with me, Kelly, you play them with yourself as well.'

'Games?' A brittle laugh. 'Heavens, Nicholas, why should I play games?'

'We both know why.'

He took a step towards her. Instinctively she moved back. Directly behind her was an oak tree; there was no chance to move aside. She was against the wide trunk of the tree, and a long arm on either side of her body blocked her escape.

'We both know, don't we?' he persisted.

It was hard to think. He was so close to her that the smell and the touch of him threatened to swamp her senses. It was only with a supreme effort of will that she managed to say, 'Do we?'

'Why didn't you tell Mary we were sharing the the cottage?'

All day she had been expecting the question. She had avoided him for that reason. The question was one which she had tried not to answer even to herself. And now Nicholas was forcing an answer from her.

Hysteria bubbled inside her. 'You made the situation so...' she struggled to find a word, and wondered if she had found the right one '...so inevitable. That being the case there was no sense in letting Mary worry. As you said, she has enough to worry about as it is.'

Laughter sounded in his throat, low and sensuous. In the circle of his arms she tensed, wondering if it was possible that he could be unaware of the thudding of her heart against her ribs. 'Nobility doesn't suit you, Kelly.'

'I merely tried to answer your question.' Damn the man! He had no right to put her in this position. 'I can't help it if you don't like it.'

'It amuses me when you resort to self-righteousness to hide the truth.'

Her chest was so tight now that it was an effort to breathe. 'I'm not hiding anything.'

'No? You're a warm-blooded female, Kelly. You might not like me very much, but you certainly are a lot more interested in sex than you'd like people to think.' Very deliberately he stepped even closer. She could feel the long hard length of his body against hers, provocative and intoxicating, and was powerless to prevent the shudder which shot through her slender frame. Another laugh, more seductive this time, revealed that her reaction had not escaped him. 'Need I say any more?' he drawled.

'I hate you!' she muttered through clenched lips.

'A positive emotion at least.' His tone was satisfied. 'Preferable any day to the lukewarm mush you dish up for Andrew Lang and that so-called fiancé of yours.'

Two balled fists managed to insert themselves between his body and hers. 'Leave me alone, Nicholas.'

'If that's what you wanted you'd have told Mary about our sleeping arrangements.'

He gave her no chance to retort. The arms which held her pinned against the tree slid behind her back, pulling her roughly to him. At the same time his mouth closed on hers. For minutes which had no meaning in time there was no rational thought. There were just the lips which probed and tasted and tantalised, the hands which descended to her hips, moulding the soft body against hard masculine lines, the smell of a potent maleness. There was the feel of a muscled chest, rough against the smoothness of bare breasts—with an expertise which Kelly hardly noticed Nicholas had slipped the dress from her shoulders—and there was the coolness of the tree's bark against her back. There was no conscious thought as Kelly's lips parted to receive Nicholas's kiss, as her arms went around his neck, pressing him even closer against her. There was only a desire that was ecstasy and agony at the same time.

After what seemed eternity the lips that probed the hollow at the base of her throat lifted. 'Say it, Kelly.' His voice was husky.

Kelly looked up through a blur. It was too dark to see the expression in the grey eyes, the features of the stern face. But she sensed the rigidity in the line of the jaw, and immediately tension knotted inside her. She could only stare at him wordlessly.

'Say it!' He demanded harshly.

'Say what?' Her bewilderment was genuine.

'That this is what you want.'

It *was* what she wanted. No use denying it—not

to herself. Not to him either. Her abandoned responses would give the lie to any denial.

'Okay,' she said flatly, 'I do want it. You're an
expert, Nicholas. You know just how to stir a
woman.' She paused a fraction of a moment before
adding the face-saver, 'But I meant what I said
about hating you.'

She felt his body stiffen. But the words that came
back to her through the darkness were spoken
lightly, sardonically. 'You must know that the line
which divides hate from love is a fine one.' And
before she could draw breath to answer, 'But that
isn't what we're talking about, is it, Kelly? We're
talking about sex. That's the name of this particular
exercise.'

She was glad that it was too dark for him to see
the tears that misted her lashes. 'You're a swine!'
she threw at him.

'For opening your eyes to the truth? Grow up,
little Kelly. Be honest with yourself. Then you'll
know why you didn't tell Mary the truth about our
sleeping arrangements.'

It was a statement of fact and they both knew
it. Kelly had been forced to admit that she was
stirred by him. In the circumstances she could
hardly have done otherwise. But painful as it had
been, she wondered if he knew that the admission
she was making in her own mind was doubly painful.

As if to push the pain from her she said, 'I'm not
sleeping with you, Nicholas.'

Another laugh, even more sensuous this time.
'What would happen if I tried to persuade you, I

wonder? I think you'd give in, Kelly.' A finger lifted to her cheek and trailed slowly, tantalisingly, down her throat and further to the hollow between her breasts. The movement brought a fresh torrent of desire coursing through Kelly's body, so that even while she wanted to push the finger from her she could not move. 'An interesting supposition, wouldn't you say?' he continued in an outrageous drawl.

With uncanny perceptiveness he had struck too near what Kelly suspected was the truth. 'No!' The word was gasped, the denial more a violent shake of the head. 'You wouldn't dare!'

'You don't know me very well if you think that? His voice was very soft now. 'I'd dare most things if I wanted them enough. It just so happens that you're safe tonight.'

'You don't want me?' The words were torn from her. She would have given much to bite them back the moment they had been uttered.

Another laugh, soft and amused and infinitely seductive. 'I won't say I like my women more willing. You're willing enough, though you want to pretend otherwise. Let's just say there are times when I prefer a degree of experience.'

'Like Serena de Jager!' Kelly choked on the name.

'Nobody could call Serena inexperienced.' There was no missing the satisfaction in his tone.

Was there an answer? Kelly did not know. If there was one she could not think of it. For his last words had given her more pain than the devastating kisses which had preceded them. She stood very still, and a tiny hammer began pounding at her temples.

Once more a long finger traced a sinuous line from cheek to throat. Then Nicholas spoke into the darkness. 'Sleep well, Kelly.'

CHAPTER NINE

CONTRARY to Nicholas's injunction she did not sleep well. Sleep was well-nigh impossible when her mind was in a turmoil which resisted all efforts at discipline, and her body ached with a racking desire which was like nothing she had ever experienced. If she slept it was fitfully.

At the first light of dawn she was awake. Peeping warily into the living-room, she saw that Nicholas was still sleeping. For long moments she watched him. The thick dark hair lay in a careless swathe across his forehead, and the mobile lips were pressed lightly together. A tanned shoulder was visible above the edge of the rug, and the top of a broad chest. It had not occurred to Kelly to wonder whether he wore pyjamas...

There was something appealing about the sleeping figure. For the first time Kelly was seeing him at a time when he was off guard and vulnerable. She was swept with a crazy urge to touch her lips against his forehead, to let her fingers feel the hardness of his shoulder.

It was with a determined wrench that she jerked her eyes from the couch and went back into the bedroom.

If he was surprised to find her already at work when he came up to the hotel he did not say so. His good-morning was crisp, matter-of-fact, with no hint of the sensuousness of the previous night. But for an odd glint in his eyes there was nothing to indicate that he even remembered what had passed between them.

There was no teasing this morning, no seductiveness. Instead he told her that the engineering convention was coming to an end, and that the men had decided on a special dinner, a kind of banquet to finalise their proceedings. Kelly would be in charge of the dinner.

She let his words wash over her, the crispness of his tone overshadowed by the impact which his physical nearness had on her always. But at his last statement she jerked up.

'Me?' It was more an exclamation than a question.

'You,' levelly.

'Oh, no, Nicholas, I can't do it!'

'You will.' It was a quiet statement.

She looked at him wordlessly for a long moment. Then she asked, 'Why, Nicholas?'

'It's something Mary would have organised if she had been here.'

'Nicholas, I . . .' She hesitated, struggling for the words that would convey her uncertainty, her feelings of inadequacy. 'This banquet will be important, a yardstick by which to measure the hotel. What if I make a mess of it?'

The eyes that studied her face were considering, assessing. Kelly had the strange feeling that Nicholas was seeing in her something entirely new, something he had not seen, or cared to see, before. Which was clearly absurd.

Then he said, 'You won't make a mess, Kelly.'

'But...'

A rare streak of warmth lit the grey eyes. As if he had not heard the beginning of her protest he went on, 'You're more competent than you think.'

She was suddenly breathless. 'You mean that, don't you?'

'Of course.' This time the warmth extended to a smile. 'You'll cope, Kelly.'

Just a few words. Coming from anyone else they were words which would have elicited no response in Kelly. But the words came from the lips of the rugged-featured man who was like nobody else she had ever known, a man who from the moment he had set eyes on her had made no secret of his dislike and contempt. The words were praise indeed.

As Nicholas left her to go on with her duties Kelly found that she was filled with a ridiculous happiness. Nicholas had shown confidence in her. He knew only too well the importance of this banquet to Great Peaks Lodge. If he was confident it could be only because he thought the feeling well founded.

It came as no surprise that this unexpected token of esteem should fill her with such elation, for she had reached a point where her own feelings could no longer be pushed from the conscious reaches of her mind. Nicholas would never love her—strange how hard it was to use the word in connection with him—he might never even learn to like her, but his confidence was a sign of a dawning respect, a sign that he was seeing her as a person with worth and value apart from her position as her father's daughter. Though she could not deny to herself that what she yearned for from Nicholas Van Mijden was something other than respect, the fact that he no longer looked at her as nothing more than a parasite with a reasonably desirable body gave a definite lift to her spirits.

She *would* cope, she vowed. Though she had never done anything quite like it before, she had been hostess at enough of her father's parties to know what was required. For the Andersons' sake she would organise the banquet as well as she knew how, so that the engineers would use the hotel as a venue again. As far as Nicholas was concerned, she would prove to him once and for all that he had misjudged her.

All that day and the next Kelly threw herself into preparing for the function. The actual cooking and setting of the tables would be done by the staff. But there was a wealth of planning to do—the menu, the placing of the tables, the flower arrangements, even some special décor. When Nicholas had first broached the subject, it had thrown her briefly into confusion. But as her planning began to take shape and form, Kelly found that she was not only gaining satisfaction from the project, she was actually enjoying herself.

Andrew sought her out more than once, and seemed disquieted that she had no time for him. Once, when the engineers had a free afternoon, he asked her to go for a walk with him. At her refusal an odd expression crossed his face—not quite resentment, Kelly decided, unconsciously seeking to put a name to it, yet something very like it. For some reason she was sorry she had chosen just that moment to look at him. Then the expression vanished, and in a friendly tone he reminded her that he would be staying on at the hotel after the convention had ended. She promised that they would have their walk then.

Now and then Nicholas appeared in the room where Kelly sat with her lists. He was interested in her plans and listened without interrupting when she explained some new idea. She did not know that her eyes were lit with radiance when she talked, or that her lips curved in a smile which transformed prettiness into beauty. She knew only that Nicholas, for the first time in their acquaintance, treated her as a person whose words were worthy of attention. Occasionally he questioned or commented, and when he did so the sardonic look was absent from his eyes, and the mockery was gone from his tone.

As always, she was affected by his presence. It seemed there was nothing she could do to quell the leaping of her senses whenever he came near her. While they talked she was conscious of the desire to reach out and touch him, to feel his arms about her body. But just as the mockery was gone from his manner, so his behaviour seemed to have become wholly platonic. It was almost as if the moments in the scent-filled garden had never been.

'Do you think Mary will be back before the banquet?' she asked once.

Something came and went in the grey eyes which regarded her with a disturbing intentness. 'I shouldn't think so.'

'No?' She could not keep the eagerness from her tone.

'You'd be sorry if she did?' There was an expres-

sion now in his face which Kelly could not define.
The closest she could get was approval, and it could
not be that. Nevertheless she felt a sudden leaping
of the senses.

'Yes.' She smiled up at him, her teeth small and
white against the tan which coloured her cheeks
after the many days in the sun. 'At this stage I'd
like to see it through all the way on my own.'

A long-fingered hand went to her hair, pushing a
loose strand gently from her forehead. It was no
more than a gesture, she knew. The hair had escaped its neat style and Nicholas was concerned
about her appearance before the hotel guests. Nonetheless it was a gesture which had the feel of a
caress. It was also the first time he had touched her
since the night in the garden, when her back had
been pressed hard against the rough bark of the oak-
tree and Nicholas had intimated that she knew
nothing of her feelings. The memory of that evening was still vivid in Kelly's mind. As if he was
holding her now, she could feel the tautness of the
hard body against hers, could smell the maleness
that was so intoxicating, could hear Nicholas taunt
her with the true reason why she had not told Mary
they were sharing a cottage. 'What would happen if
I tried to persuade you to sleep with me?' he had
asked. More and more she thought she knew the
answer to that question. As a tremor shot through
her body she lowered her eyes quickly beneath long
lashes.

'You'll see it through.' Nicholas's voice was low
and amused. Kelly had the disturbing feeling that
he knew exactly what she had been thinking.

'Try and stop me!'

And they smiled at each other, a real smile for the very first time since they had known each other, before going their separate ways.

The banquet was a success. Everything went according to plan. The meal was different from the one the chefs would have prepared had they been left to themselves, but once Kelly had explained what she wanted they were more than willing to follow her instructions. The bowls and tubs of flowers placed unobtrusively yet strategically around the big room added an exotic touch, and the décor, much of which Kelly had designed herself, elicited more than a few compliments. Best of all, when the function was over the convention chairman approached Kelly and Nicholas who happened to be standing together, and told them that he would ensure that the following year's convention would again be at Great Peaks Lodge.

'That's good news,' Nicholas said. His words were addressed to the engineer, but his eyes were on Kelly, and the expression that she saw there sent a warm flush cascading through her cheeks.

There was no chance to talk further to Nicholas, for just then Andrew came from behind and put his hand on her arm. In a way she was glad. Any words she could have exchanged with Nicholas at that point could have only been an anticlimax.

It was late when Kelly went at last to the cottage. Nicholas was nowhere to be seen. In a sense she was disappointed, for it seemed she would not see him again that night. Yet in another sense she was re-

lieved. The day had been so perfect that she wanted
nothing to spoil it. Too often in the past Nicholas
had been sarcastic or mocking, finding a vulner-
ability where she had not known it existed. After
the banquet there had been a look in his eyes which
she had never seen there before. When she lay in
bed and relived the events of the day she meant to
cherish that look, to hug it to her, as it were. It was
the final touch to a day she would never forget.

'Sleepyhead!' There was a gentle quality in the
tone which made it seem, through the blur of sleep,
unfamiliar. And then, as her mind came to full wak-
ing consciousness, Kelly's eyes snapped open.

'Nicholas!' It was very light in the room—clearly
she had slept later than usual—but Nicholas did
not seem to mind. There was a look of amusement
in his face, mixed with a quality which in any other
man she might have taken for tenderness.

'I overslept,' she said softly.

'You certainly did!'

'I'm sorry about that. You should have woken
me.'

Now the mockery would come, the stinging remark which could wound as well as excite.
Strangely the unfamiliar expression in his eyes
deepened instead. 'You earned your sleep, Kelly.'

And now it was all rushing back—the memory of
the banquet, the wonderful moment when the
chairman of the convention had said the hotel
would be used again next year; the memory of
Nicholas's approval of the way she had handled the

affair, an approval which had been implied if it had not been put into words.

She had not heard him enter the cottage. She had lain in her bed, going over every minute of the evening, and had wondered when he would come. She had thought she would never sleep, but clearly she had. Nicholas must have gone to bed very late. What had he been doing? Had he sat talking to the engineers, or had he been attending to some facet of the hotel's running? A late-night rendezvous perhaps with Serena de Jager? Yesterday just the thought would have been enough to give Kelly pain. But today, with the sun streaming in through the windows, and with Nicholas standing over her with that disturbing look in his eyes, it did not seem to matter.

'Let me get dressed,' she said, glancing towards the door in a hint that he should leave the room. 'I'm way behind with my tasks.'

'No tasks today.' At her astonishment he chuckled, the sound low and sensuous and very seductive. 'You've earned more than your sleep, Kelly. You've earned a day off—we both have.'

She stared at him, and wondered if he knew that her spirits had plummeted. A day off? A day to explore the gardens or take a walk along one of the easier mountain trails. A day alone. Andrew would be busy with last-minute activities, and Nicholas would spend the precious leisure time with Serena. The idea of a day off was unappealing.

'That's nice,' she said brightly. 'I'll walk down to the river. I might even lie by the pool all day and just bake in the sun.'

That would provoke the mockery, she thought. But once more his reaction surprised her. 'You know you'd be bored to tears.' At her incredulous gasp his teeth flashed in a brief smile, strong and white and wicked against the tan of his skin. 'You'll spend the day with me, Kelly. At my plantation.'

It was a blue and golden day. The mountain peaks were free of mist. The air rang with the sound of bird-song, and through the open window of Nicholas's car came the aromatic scent of the veld flowers. Small brown-skinned children danced at the roadside, waving and smiling as the car slowed to pass them, and once a wild foal turned a startled head before vanishing in the long grass of the underbrush.

The mountain road was narrow and winding, but Nicholas took the hairpin bends with an ease which did not surprise Kelly. Nothing this man could do would surprise her, and excitement mounted within her at the thought of seeing his home. When he had told her that they would spend the day together she had been filled with a happiness which she had tried hard to conceal. For it would not do to let Nicholas know quite how much the idea of being alone with him, away from duties and obligations, meant to her. He would mock her, would remind her of Gary, and make a sarcastic reference to the fact that her fiancé did not know what she did when she was away from him.

Her fiancé ... Her shoulders stiffened and a frown creased her forehead. 'We must think about things,' she had told him. Gary must be wondering about her decision. She owed him an answer. She knew already what the answer would be, but she would put it to him gently. What she would not tell him was the thoroughness with which Nicholas had succeeded in surplanting him in her thoughts and in her dreams. That was something which Kelly herself, on leaving Great Peaks Lodge, would have to do her utmost to forget. For if she did not, the years ahead would hold only unhappiness.

With an effort she tried to force her concentration back to the loveliness of the passing countryside. If she was going to spend the day brooding she would spoil things not only for Nicholas but also for herself. Kelly wanted very badly to enjoy this day. It would be part of a memory—there was no way she could hide the knowledge from herself—a memory of a time which had been very important to her, a time which would always linger in the secret reaches of her mind as one of the most memorable she had known.

For a while the road ran beside a narrow stream. There were no bends ahead, and no traffic. Some instinct told Kelly that Nicholas was watching her. She turned from the window and met his gaze. Grey eyes were lit by a warmth which made him look more human than she had seen him, his lips were curved in a slight smile, making her wonder at the cause of his amusement. A fawn sports shirt clung to the contours of a muscled chest, revealing broad shoulders, and from the open collar his throat rose strong and tanned. There was never a time when Kelly was unaffected by the sheer impact of the man, an impact that was basic and primeval and thoroughly devastating in its intensity. Colour washed her cheeks as an answering chord struck deep within her, shattering her with the raw desire to reach out and touch him. She longed to move across the seat where her shoulder and hip and thigh could rest against his. With difficulty she swallowed, and saw the smile deepen.

'Enjoy today, Kelly.' The words, so quietly spoken, were nevertheless in the nature of a command.

'I will,' she said a little breathlessly as she turned back to the window, unable to sustain the gaze which registered soft flushed cheeks and radiant wide eyes and the little pulse which beat frenziedly in the hollow of a slender neck.

They came at length to Pinevale. All around were the forests. Acres upon acres of healthy-looking trees. Kelly had imagined that the forest reserves were all state property. In the main she was right, Nicholas told her, but here and there a private plantation existed, and Pinevale was one of them.

She listened attentively as he told her about the lands, about the trees and the sawmills and the innovations he had made. Now and then she asked a question, and her questions must have been intelligent, for he answered seriously and with due consideration. Not for nothing was Kelly Robert Stanwick's daughter. She quickly grasped the magnitude of responsibility and foresight involved in an operation of this size, and had only respect for the man who had the energy and the dedication to control it.

But even greater than her interest was her joy in

hearing him talk. While she had hated the mockery and the arrogance to which she had been subjected until so recently, she had suspected that Nicholas must also possess other qualities. She had glimpsed his gentleness with Mary, and the quiet friendliness in his dealings with people he liked, though she had doubted she would ever see these qualities applied to herself.

As they drove between the forested slopes of Pinevale, she was seeing a new Nicholas. The power and authority were still there, coupled with the intoxicating maleness. But as if he had dropped a mask which he no longer needed, he now allowed Kelly to see his love for the land, his dedication to the plantation he had built up, the intensity of his feeling for the place which was his home.

This was how she must remember him, Kelly thought, as she listened to Nicholas talk. Today would give her an insight into the man who had made more impact on her than anyone she had ever met. It would also give substance to the memory of the man she loved.

For she loved Nicholas. Useless to deny the fact to herself. Until yesterday she had tried to push the knowledge from her mind, for it was a love without any future. Nicholas Van Mijden was the one man who would never return her feelings. He did not like her, had never liked her. And his marriage to Serena could be only a matter of time.

There was so much to see at Pinevale, so much to marvel at. Kelly had realised very soon that whatever Nicholas did he would do well, but she had not expected quite the degree of lushness and expanse which now met her eyes. It had puzzled her at the beginning that he treated her so differently from all the other men she had known. Now she was puzzled no longer. It was not in Nicholas Van Mijden to fawn upon someone else. This would hold true no matter what his position might be in the world. He was master of himself and proud of it, a state of mind that was not governed by riches or status or the lack of them both. It just so happened that Nicholas *was* in fact a man of great wealth. Kelly had only to look around her to know that.

Emerging from the forests they came to a long winding drive which led to the homestead. Set in a cleft between the folds of two wooded hills, Kelly thought the house one of the loveliest she had ever seen. It was long and low, with great picture windows which sparkled like polished diamonds where the sun caught the glass, and creepers which trailed and climbed in a soaring thrust towards the thatched roof. Kelly saw that the house had been built so that the view from the main windows was into the mountains. She thought of Nicholas sitting in the late afternoon on the patio, relaxing after the work of the day, with a dog by his side and a glass of cold beer in his hand. She could imagine him looking towards the mountains, watching the colours of the sunset turn the high peaks from scarlet to gold and at last to a mysterious shade that was somewhere between yellow and grey. The picture was vivid, and for no reason at all a lump formed in her throat.

Then a new figure entered the picture: Serena.

Poised and cool and beautiful, in a chair by Nicholas's side, listening as he told her all that happened that day. And added to the lump in Kelly's throat came a dull pain beneath her ribs which was becoming all too familiar.

There was no time to brood, for already Nicholas was leading her across a thick carpet of lawn towards the wide stone steps that led on to the patio.

Just as the house was the very antithesis of Kelly's idea of a bachelor's domain, so she imagined the rooms would be different too. That they would be well furnished she expected—Nicholas Van Mijden was a man who would never be content with second best—but she was curious to discover the actual nature of his tastes. When he asked if she would like a tour of the house she accepted with alacrity. Just for a moment the grey eyes gleamed with satisfaction, and it came to Kelly that he wanted her to see his home just as much as she wanted to see it. The reason was not hard to find. Nicholas was proud of his home. It would give him pleasure to let people see it—there could be nothing more to it than that. And yet the warmth lighting the dark eyes filled her with a breathless kind of happiness.

As they went from one room to another, Kelly saw how Nicholas had made the most of the house and its setting. Lovely Persian rugs were scattered on the polished oak floor, and much of the furniture was antique. The woods were African, stinkwood and teak and a fine-grained mahogany, each piece with a sheen which indicated love and care and pride of possession.

In contrast, the curtains and cushions were light-coloured and modern, well chosen to blend quite naturally with the dark woods, brightening the rooms and giving them a sense of space and colour appropriate to the rustic mountain setting.

'Well?' Nicholas asked from behind her, when Kelly turned from admiring a Pierneef landscape that dominated one wide wall, gracing the dining-room with the master painter's touch.

'It's all so beautiful.' Her voice was low, and she wondered if he could hear her breathlessness. She wanted to ask if someone had helped in the furnishing of the house—Serena perhaps?—but it was a question she could not frame, not when he stood so near to her that she was aware of every inch of the virile male body.

'I'm glad.' He spoke very simply. For once there was neither mockery nor amusement in his expression. Just a deepening of the satisfaction which she had glimpsed a little earlier. That in itself was no cause for notice, and yet, inexplicably, the adrenalin shot through her nerve-stream.

'Want to see more?' He asked with a hint of teasing.

The master bedroom—it could only be that. She wanted to see it so badly that she had to conceal her eyes beneath long dark lashes, for otherwise their expression would have been fatally easy to read. No, was what she should have said. It was the only correct reply in the circumstances. But sometimes, particularly when one's heartbeat is doing funny things inside one's chest, words have a trick of coming out differently from the way they should.

'Yes,' she said simply.

CHAPTER TEN

THE room was large. It was also simply but tastefully furnished. Kelly did not take in the actual objects in the room so much as the atmosphere. It was basic and strong and male, much like its owner. Even while her senses assimilated the overall impression, another thought came to mind—without much difficulty the bedroom could be adapted into one which a woman would enjoy sharing.

As if to erase the thought, Kelly shook her head. The movement did not escape Nicholas.

'You don't like the room, Kelly?' His voice was very soft. To Kelly's fevered imagination it seemed to hold a deep undercurrent of meaning.

'Like?' She turned to him, unaware that her eyes were naked with the rawness of her emotions. 'Oh, yes!'

'Kelly...' He had taken a step towards her. His eyes were very dark, a tiny muscle worked in his jaw, and his long limbs seemed tauter than she had ever seen them.

Did she meet him half-way? Later she could not have put into words what happened. There was just the meeting of two bodies, the soft feminine one crushed against the hardness of the tall male one, and as he kissed her time ceased to have any meaning. His lips were hard and demanding, but in place of the punishment she had experienced on occasion there was a passion which indicated the depth of his desire. His hands were light and tantalising, strong and sensual, all at the same time, caressing and exploring and moulding her to him.

Kelly was swept by a torrent of desire that was stronger than anything she had ever known. There was no thought now, no moralising on what was right and what was wrong. There was just the wish, which superseded all else, to be close to this man, ever closer, part of him ... There was no thought as she slid her arms beneath his shirt. There was just glory in the feel of the muscles which tightened beneath her fingers, in the knowledge that she wanted him.

She did not protest as he lifted her on to the bed. With an unsuspected tenderness he took the clothes from her body, and then began to undress himself. His eyes never left her face. He did not ask any questions. None were needed; the longing in her eyes spoke for itself.

As he came towards her she reached out her arms. Her lips were parted to reveal tiny white teeth against the apricot tan of her skin, and a pulse beat a feverish tattoo in the little hollow at the base of her throat. Her breasts were firm and round, and she made no attempt to cover them with her hands. There was no embarrassment, no thought of shame. There was only the knowledge that she loved Nicholas. If there was also the knowledge that she could have no future with him, she did not dwell on it consciously. There was only the desire to be with him as a woman is with the man she loves more than life itself.

'Kelly.' The word emerged in the form of a groan. Coming from this strong and self-sufficient man the sound was strangely moving. 'Kelly, do you know what you're doing to me?'

'Yes...' No more than a whisper.

'You're so lovely.' He sank down on to the bed and gathered her to him. His hands moved over her shoulders, her back, her hips, moulding her un-resistant body to his.

He began to kiss her again, his lips a sweet tor-ture against eyes and throat and breasts. Her nostrils were filled with the smell of his maleness, and each one of her senses was vibrantly alive.

'There can be no turning back,' he said once, lifting his head.

'I know.' Only dimly was she aware of the possible consequences of their lovemaking. Her senses had taken over her body, destroying the last vestiges of any resistance, but that did not seem to matter.

'Kelly ...' This time the voice was huskier than before. 'If only you knew how I...'

A loud ringing invaded the room, shocking, some-how obscene. It took a second for Kelly to under-stand that it was the ring of the telephone.

'Damn!' Nicholas swore quietly.

'Don't answer...' Kelly uttered an unashamed plea.

The telephone rang once more, unheeded, as a rough hand caressed a smooth shoulder. Then Nicholas lifted himself away from her. 'I must. It must be urgent for Joshua to put the call through.'

Kelly lay rigid on the bed and watched as he cradled the receiver to his ear. His breathing was still a little ragged, and she was so close to him that she imagined she could hear the quickened beat of his heart. But his tone was terse and clipped, so that the person at the other end of the line could have had no idea of what he had interrupted.

'Kelly, I'm needed ...' The conversation ended, he replaced the phone and looked down at the small feminine figure.

'Nicholas, I ... Can't ...' She paused, uncertain and unhappy, the words refusing to come.

'Perhaps it's better this way.' The mobile lips curved wryly, and there was a strange tenderness in the eyes which studied the flushed oval face. A hand touched a breast, lingering fleetingly before trailing a path up the slender column of the throat. Kelly held her breath, the sensual touch giving her an exquisite pleasure which transcended all need for words.

'Maybe the call was providential.' The huskiness in his voice gave the lie to his smile. 'I couldn't have stopped, Kelly. You know that.'

Through a blur of pain she watched him get dressed. The telephone had prevented him from making love to her fully. He was glad, Kelly thought, he had said almost as much. It was only a thoughtless intimacy which had provoked his emotions to blind passion. But he did not want her, not really. Now that he had a few moments to reflect on what had happened he was clear about that, whereas she wanted him more than she had ever wanted anything in her life.

'I'm needed at the mill.' His breathing had quietened. 'Would you like to come with me, or would you rather relax in the garden for a while?'

She had pulled the sheet over her. For the timeless moments when only passion had existed, there had been no embarrassment. Now she did not want him to see her unclothed. 'If you wait for me I'll come along.' She tried to make her voice as casual as his. Not for anything should he guess at the turmoil raging within her. 'The mill is part of the general tour, isn't it?'

An enigmatic expression appeared in his eyes. Perhaps he guessed at her pain, yet was glad that she would regard what had happened as no more than the interlude it had been meant to be.

'Get dressed,' he said quietly. 'I'll wait for you on the patio.'

What were his thoughts as he waited? Kelly wondered, as she showered in the chocolate-tiled bathroom before slipping into her clothes. Did he see her as a girl without any morals? A girl who enjoyed taking her fun behind her fiancé's back? If he did, it would not surprise him. Nicholas's opinion of her had been low from the start. He had seen her only as a spoiled parasite who had bribed a man in order to fulfil a whim. He had taken pleasure in getting her to work off a debt, never dreaming that she gained an enormous satisfaction from what she did. This new evidence of her character would merely strengthen his views.

Even with Gary's ring on her finger Kelly had not been prepared to share a room with him. Yet she had yearned to experience Nicholas's lovemaking to the fullest. The reason for this was simple, but Nicholas would never know it. For she could not tell him that she loved him, nor that she understood for the first time how a woman could be stirred to a point where reasoning took second place to emotion.

This was a love which she had never experienced with Gary. Had she not decided to end her engagement because she could no longer accept the immature aspects of her fiancé's nature, Kelly knew that she would in any case have had to change her mind about marrying him. What she had once felt for Gary was no more than infatuation for a man who was totally different from the people who moved in her father's world of high finance.

Her feelings for Nicholas were on another level altogether. Though there could be no future with him, she did not regret the time at Great Peaks. For she knew now that she was a woman in every sense of the word and that it was in her to love very deeply. For some reason that was important. She would never see Nicholas again—there was no way she would revisit this part of the Drakensberg to reopen a wound whose rawness she could only hope would lessen with time—yet Kelly knew that wherever life might take her, she would never forget the magic days when she had crossed the threshold into emotional womanhood.

She came on to the patio and found him waiting for her. His back was to the doorway, and he was staring over the pine-covered slopes of the plantation. And then he turned, and there was a remoteness in his eyes before which she froze.

When he had dealt with the situation in the sawmill, an important one which revealed to Kelly how much he had sacrificed in giving up his time to supervise the running of the hotel, Nicholas showed her around. Everywhere there was activity, and the men who worked in the mill were openly glad to see him. The sawmill was well run, its operations efficient, each man understood his function. Yet all looked to Nicholas for direction. It was as if he gave a focus to their working lives. As he was fast becoming the focus of her own life, Kelly thought.

Throughout he was polite. Kelly could not fault him on that. A stranger might even have thought him friendly. But the remoteness never left his manner. To Kelly, who had shared moments of the closest sensual intimacy with this man, the remoteness was more painful than all his previous mockery and contempt had been.

She was almost glad when they returned at last to Great Peaks Lodge. She had had such high hopes for this day. For a short time it had even seemed as if she would experience an ecstasy greater than anything she had ever imagined. And then suddenly, inexplicably, the magic of the day was gone, and in its place was a numbing emptiness.

Had she done something wrong? she wondered. Had she offended him in some way? Twice she parted dry lips to ask him a question. But a glance at his profile, detached and a little forbidding, stifled the words before they were uttered.

Serena was at Great Peaks for dinner that evening. Kelly did not know if she had been invited by Nicholas or if he was surprised by her coming. Even without the presence of the cool poised beauty the meal would have been a strain. But with Serena at

the table, claiming and receiving Nicholas's un-
divided attention, it would be unbearable. Kelly had
no qualms about excusing herself from dinner. She
had had a long day at Pinevale, she said, and was
tired. She would have an early night.

At mention of Pinevale Serena's glance went
quickly to Nicholas. For the first time she looked
uncertain of herself. But Kelly gained no satisfaction from what was only a very minor and, in the
circumstances, meaningless victory. Her head was
aching as she walked through the scent-filled garden to the cottage.

For a while she lay on the Andersons' big double
bed. The light was off and as she stared through the
open window she tried very hard to relax, a difficult
feat when just a little distance away, in the candlelit intimacy of the dining-room, Serena was en-
chanting Nicholas with her loveliness. What would
that woman say if she knew of the scene in the bedroom at Pinevale? Kelly wondered. Would she
mind very much? Would she ache with a pain that
knifed beneath the ribs and throbbed at the
temples?—a pain which Kelly was beginning to
know too well. The thought was an idle one.
Nicholas would never tell his bride-to-be what had
happened. Apart from the fact that he would not
want to disturb Serena, there was no reason for him
to mention an incident which had been of no importance to him.

The breeze which wafted in through the window
did not lessen the heat in the room. Kelly moved
restlessly on the bed. Though she was not tired in a
physical sense, she wanted very much to sleep. Sleep

would block out thought, it would block out the turmoil of emotion which she had never imagined when she left Gary and his friends in Estcourt to return to Great Peaks Lodge.

How differently things had turned out from the way she had planned them, she mused wryly. Helping out at Great Peaks had been an unexpected development, but it had been one to which she had quickly adjusted. Falling in love was something else altogether. This she had not anticipated, had not wanted—still did not want. She had not yet found a way of coping with the event which had changed her world so that it would never be quite the same again. She wondered now if she ever would.

Impatient all at once, she left the bed and went out of the cottage. Outside the air was aromatic and cool. Save for the ceaseless hum of the crickets it was very still. As she walked through the quiet garden, Kelly felt a little of the tension draining from her.

Silently she moved between the dark shapes of the trees, her footfalls deadened by the thickness of the grass. She saw Nicholas quite suddenly. There was no mistaking the broad shoulders and the tall well-built body; the tilt of the head and the thrust of the throat. There was no mistaking her own instinctive reaction, the tightening of her muscles and the instant leaping of her senses. Pride forgotten— what did it matter if Serena had had dinner with him?—Kelly stepped quickly forwards. And then, just as suddenly, she checked the movement.

For Nicholas was not alone. The breadth of his shoulders had blocked the vision of someone else but now that person had moved just a little, and Kelly saw the white folds of a dress brush against the long male trouser-legs.

She stood still as a statue. Through the quiet air came the sound of Serena's voice, brittle and not as poised as she remembered it, and then the low answering tone of the man with whom she stood. Kelly could not hear their actual words, and did not want to. She wanted only to leave the scene before they saw her. She would have fled if her limbs had not been suddenly robbed of the power of movement.

As she watched, Nicholas bent his head, and two slender arms came up to clasp themselves behind his neck. Kelly choked back an involuntary sob. Blood surged back through her limbs. As the couple not more than a few yards from her clung together in an embrace, she vanished, like a wounded animal, away through the trees.

She was still awake when Nicholas came into the cottage. She lay quietly in the bed that belonged to the Andersons, and when he opened the door of her room and came towards her bed she made her breathing slow and deep. For what seemed a long time he stood beside her. He did not speak—the regularity of her breathing must have had him convinced—and she was thankful that it was too dark for him to see the matted lashes and the moist patch on her pillow.

Even now, when she had every reason to hate him, Kelly was acutely aware of the long virile body and the clean male smell that seemed to fill the room. She heard him take a step away from the bed, and then he halted. A hand touched her hair, the movement like a caress. At the touch her chest tightened. It became an effort to breathe at all. Just as she wondered how long she could keep up her act, the hand left her hair, and she heard him walk from the room. His footsteps had a sound that was quick and angry.

She became adept at avoiding him. Avoidance was important. If the wound that slashed her emotions were to heal at all, the less contact she had with Nicholas the better. Kelly had grown accustomed to the daily routine of the hotel. She did not need Nicholas to guide or advise her. She knew too his own routine. It was relatively easy to keep out of his way. And Mary *must* return soon...

When Andrew asked her to go for a walk with him she accepted with alacrity. The invitation came at a time when her chores were done and she was at a loss for something to kill the hours until lunch.

They took a path that swung around the hotel towards a mountain cleft where the slopes were covered in jungle. Trees, tall and spindly, reached for the sun through a dense green canopy of foliage. Roots sprawled grotesquely above the ground, and moss and toadstools made a spongy carpet underfoot.

Although from the beginning Andrew had made a point of seeking her out, they had never been quite alone together. Kelly found herself enjoying the walk. After the strain of the last few days it was refreshing to be able to relax in a man's company. So much had happened since the day they had met

that she had almost forgotten the occasional under-
tone and the look which had been sometimes in Andrew's eyes. She only knew that she liked this man
very much, and that it was fun to be with him in the
dim coolness of the jungle.

They came to a waterfall where the water spilled
over the wet cliff-face to fall into the measureless
depths of a dark pool. Wild lilies grew at the edge
of the pool, and a thin shaft of light speared
the jungle canopy, splintering the water into tiny
prisms of light.

'Isn't this beautiful!' Kelly uttered the words on
an indrawn breath of sheer delight.

'*You* are beautiful.'

Kelly turned slowly, caught by the inflection in
Andrew's tone. She had been smiling, but now the
smile trembled on her lips as she met his gaze.

'Andrew ...' Her tone was low, the name spoken
in a kind of warning. The expression in his face
told her what she should have anticipated. But even
now perhaps it was not too late ...

'Kelly.' His tone was equally low, and the sound
of her name was a caress. Two hands reached for
her shoulders, drawing her to him. 'Kelly, you must
know how I feel about you.'

'Don't, Andrew. Please!' She blinked back sudden tears. There was urgency in the hands that held
her, and in her new-found womanhood Kelly knew
what it was to be hurt.

'I must.'

This was a new Andrew, this man who gathered
her to him despite her resistance, his arms hard—
though not as hard as Nicholas's—and his lips

passionate. After a moment Kelly gave up the effort to resist. She liked Andrew; she liked him very much. And if she could allow herself to be stirred by his touch then perhaps, after all, she was not quite lost.

Putting her arms around his neck, she tried to respond to his kiss. It took her just a moment to know that she could not do it. Andrew was probably the nicest man she knew, but physically he left her unmoved.

As if he sensed her feelings, he drew away. 'It's no good, is it?' His voice was level.

'No.' She whispered.

'It's still Gary?'

She could not answer the question. It was not fair of him to expect it. But there was integrity in the clear eyes that studied hers, and despite his hurt there was no trace of the resentment a lesser man might well have shown.

She shook her head. The movement was painful.

'Then it's Nicholas.' Kelly had not known Andrew could be quite so hard. 'There's no future with the man, Kelly.'

'I know ...'

'I love you, Kelly. I could give you so much.'

She swallowed on the lump in her throat. 'I couldn't give you anything in return.'

He hesitated a moment, then he said, 'You'd be my wife.'

'You wouldn't want me without my love.' She looked at him, the tears shimmering on long lashes. 'You deserve more, Andrew.'

He did not press her, and for that she was glad. The walk back was silent and strained. But by the time they came to the hotel Kelly had resolved certain issues in her mind.

She was sorry that she had hurt Andrew, truly sorry. But there was a look in Andrew's eyes which suggested that he had not reached his thirties without learning how to adjust to painful situations. Most likely, when he met a girl who would return his love, Kelly would become no more than a memory.

There was Gary. She had known for a while now that she could not marry him. It was not fair to keep him waiting any longer for her decision. The time had come to be honest with him. Any resentment on his part would be justified, and for that Kelly would not blame him. But even Gary had a stubborn resilience. She wondered now whether he had ever really loved her in the true sense of the word. If not, what he would suffer was essentially hurt pride and from that he would recover. With his dashing good looks and sparkling manner he would soon be sweeping another girl off her feet.

That left Nicholas, and he was a complication only as far as she herself was concerned, for his own emotions had never been in any way involved. Since the evening in the garden, when she had caught him kissing Serena, Kelly had avoided him, but the pain had not lessened. If anything, it had increased. There was only one remedy. It was time to give serious thought to the life she meant to lead on leaving Great Peaks. She needed a career which

would give her fulfilment, for she doubted now
that she would ever marry.

She thought of the many hours she had spent at
the hospital, playing with children who were ill
and unhappy, hours which had given her a certain feeling of achievement and satisfaction. As a
pastime it had been rewarding, but the pastime
was no longer enough. For a career to fill her life
it must hold a challenge. She wondered now if
nursing might provide what she sought. Soon she
would be in Durban, and there she would set about
finding out what she needed to know.

'You'll have something to drink?' Andrew asked
as they approached the verandah. It was the first
time he had spoken since leaving the waterfall.

'I don't think so.' Kelly managed a smile. She
saw that the eyes that met hers were sad but steady.
'Thanks anyway, Andrew, but it's better this way.'

'Perhaps you're right.' He reached for her hand.
'You're a very lovely girl, Kelly. I hope some day
you'll find happiness.'

He drew her to him, gently this time, and kissed
her upturned mouth. There was nothing sexual in
the kiss; the gesture was simply one of friendship
and farewell. Without another word he released her
and walked away.

'Very touching!'

Kelly spun round at the sound of the mocking
voice. At sight of sardonic eyes in a lean tanned face
she felt the colour drain from her cheeks.

'So this is how you spend your time.' His voice
was hard.

'Where I go and with whom is my own choice!'

She flung the words at him angrily, her eyes un-
naturally bright against the sudden pallor of her
face.

A hand shot out to seize her wrist. 'I want to
speak to you, Kelly.'

'No!' Despite the tremor which shuddered
through her at his touch, she managed to jerk from
his grip.

His eyes were dark strips of flint. 'Kelly . . .'

'Leave me alone, Nicholas!' Her heart was
pounding as she wondered if he would use his
greater strength to detain her. But he made no
move to stop her as she pushed past him and walked
quickly into the hotel.

She went directly to the telephone. No sense in
delaying any longer. She reached Gary without
any difficulty. The call was short. He listened
quietly as she told him her decision. Kelly guessed
that her words came as no surprise, and wondered
if Gary, in his own way, was relieved that the engagement was over. Perhaps he too had realised that
there was not enough between them to hold a marriage together. When they said goodbye Kelly found
it surprisingly hard to choke back a sob. If she had
not loved Gary, she had nevertheless liked him very
much. The conversation had taken more of a toll
on her emotions than she had anticipated.

When she had put down the phone she went to
the cottage. It was almost midday, and she would
be expected in the kitchen, but the last hour had
been so draining that she needed to be alone for a
while.

Sitting down on the Andersons' double bed, she

drew off her engagement ring. She remembered how happy she had been when Gary had placed it on her finger. Now, such a short time later, their relationship was ended, she was in love with someone else, and was poised on the brink of a career which would include neither one of the men who had played such important parts in her life.

She looked at the ring a few moments before slipping it into her purse. No point in posting it back to Gary—it might get lost. She would take it with her when she returned to Durban, and return it to him then.

Kelly was on her way to the kitchens when she paused in the doorway of the cottage. Thoughtfully she lifted her left hand. The third finger looked bare without the diamond.

Nicholas would notice that the ring had gone. As much as she was determined to keep out of his way, there would be moments when she could not help meeting him, and when she would be unable to hide her hand. There would be probing and questions. Even if Kelly refused to answer, Nicholas was too perceptive not to guess at the truth. It was a truth which Kelly did not want him to learn, at least not yet. Not until she had left Great Peaks and was away from eyes that could read more than a tumultuous heart wanted him to know.

The diamond was back on her finger when she went into the kitchens. It sparkled under the bright lights, and it seemed to Kelly as if it winked at her in mocking disdain. But she kept the ring on. No matter that the diamond was no more than a charade, and that she no longer had the right to wear

it. What was important was that Nicholas Van Mijden would not know that her engagement was
ended. For if he did, his pity would be more than
Kelly could endure.

Mary and George Anderson returned to Great Peaks
Lodge one morning late in March. Autumn was in
the air. The leaves were turning russet on the
trees, and the sky was overcast. There was a bleakness to the day, a bleakness which was echoed in
Kelly's heart. It was almost a month since the day
when George had been carried down the mountain, an unconscious figure on a swaying stretcher.

George looked well, Kelly thought—surprisingly
well. But for a limp when he walked, there was
nothing to indicate that he had had an accident
and had spent weeks in hospital. Mary too looked
very different from the last time Kelly had seen
her. Both Andersons had colour in their cheeks, and
their faces were lightly tanned. A stranger might
have thought they had been on holiday.

They were delighted to be back, and impressed
with the way Kelly had coped in their absence.
Mary begged Kelly to return to the hotel for a
holiday. 'Some time,' Kelly said smilingly, but she
knew that she would never come back to Great
Peaks Lodge.

Nicholas had missed the Andersons' return. He
had gone to Pinevale for the morning, and was not
expected back before lunch. Kelly hoped to be gone
before then. Since their last encounter she had managed, somehow, to keep her manner towards him
outwardly detached and cool. But she quailed be-

fore the prospect of saying goodbye. Such was the
pain that wrenched inside her at the knowledge that
she would never see Nicholas again, that she
doubted if will-power alone would be sufficient to
preserve the image of remoteness she had so carefully created.

As soon as she could politely do so, Kelly went to
the cottage to pack. Andrew had left a few days
earlier, so only the goodbyes to the staff, of whom
she had grown very fond, still remained. A touring
bus was leaving the hotel, and at her request George
arranged that she could go with it.

Her packing took longer than she had expected.
Now and then Kelly paused to look around her. She
had grown attached to the little cottage, in particular to the bedroom which the Andersons would
once again sleep in themselves. The room was one
which Kelly would always remember, for it was
here that she had lived through love and hate and
sorrow and excitement, and finally through a numbing disappointment which it would take her a long
time to forget.

She was closing her suitcase when she heard someone at the outer door of the cottage. Mary, she
thought, come to see how she was getting on. And
then there was the sound of impatient footsteps on
the living-room floor, and even before the bedroom
door opened the blood was pounding like a jack-
hammer in Kelly's veins.

'So.' Nicholas stood in the open doorway, tall and
sleek and dangerous in dark tight-fitting trousers
and a polo-necked sweater.

A small tongue went out to lick lips that had

gone suddenly dry. 'N-Nicholas! I ... I thought you were at Pinevale.'

'Is that why you decided to make such a quick getaway? I believe Mary couldn't even persuade you to stay for lunch.'

'I ... There's a bus leaving. I thought I might as well go back with it, and ...' She stopped, helpless before the wrath that glittered in the dark eyes.

'You also thought you could go away without seeing me.' He finished the sentence for her.

She swallowed. 'I would have said goodbye.'

'Don't lie to me, Kelly.' His voice was like ice, and the glint in his eyes was ominous. 'You meant to slip away without a word, as if there'd been nothing between us.'

'Was there something?' she countered too swiftly.

An enigmatic expression came and went in his face as he studied her. She suspected that he missed neither her agitation nor the excitement surging like a river of fire through her system.

'I thought there was,' he drawled softly. 'I seem to recall a moment when only the sound of a telephone saved what some might call your virtue. You would have slept with me, Kelly, and we both know it.'

The words were out before she could stop them. 'That was before I saw you and Serena kissing...' She clapped a hand to her mouth, and the eyes that stared at him above white-knuckled fingers were wide and green and aghast.

'So you saw us. That explains a lot.' Unaccountably the expression in the grey eyes changed.

There was a look which, in a less feverish state, Kelly might have taken for understanding. She heard him laugh. The sound was different from anything she had heard before, sensuous still, but rough too and a little husky. Then he was taking a step towards her, and she could not retreat, for behind her was the bed.

'Where are you off to now?' he demanded.

'To Durban...'

'To Gary?'

She dropped her eyes. 'Yes.'

A hand went to her chin, roughly jerking it up. 'Another lie, Kelly!' he grated harshly.

'I ... I'm not lying.' It was increasingly difficult to force the words from her parched throat.

'You are.' A thumb began a slow movement along the slender column of her throat, stopping abruptly in the hollow where the pulse beat too quickly. 'Your own special built-in lie-detector.' Nicholas's voice had softened just a fraction. 'You're not going to Gary, Kelly—I don't need your pulse rate to tell me that. You'd never be happy with the fellow. Just as you wouldn't have been happy with Andrew.'

An unreasoning happiness swept her mind. No matter that in a few minutes she would be saying goodbye to Nicholas, never to see him again. This moment was precious. It belonged only to them both. Serena and Gary had no part in it.

'How do you know?' she asked softly.

He studied her intensely for a few seconds. Once more the thumb traced a tantalising movement from shoulder to chin, its sensuousness sending a wildness to the green eyes that met grey ones with unusual courage.

'How?' A short laugh. 'Because I've come to know you, Kelly Stanwick. You're not the spoiled little rich girl I took you to be. And I know that men like Gary Sloan and Andrew would never satisfy you.' A commanding urgency entered his tone. 'I ask you again ... are you going to Gary, Kelly? I insist on the truth.'

There was a look in the rugged-featured face so close to hers which defied any attempt to continue the fiction. Strangely, the urge to conceal the facts from Nicholas had vanished.

'No.' Now her voice was very calm. 'I'm not going to Gary.'

A muscle tightened in the long line of the jaw, but his expression did not change. 'And the reason?' he asked quietly. 'The real reason, Kelly?'

She did not conceal her eyes. They were easy to read, she knew, but even that no longer seemed to matter. 'Because I love you,' she said huskily.

'Kelly ...' The break in the vibrant masculine voice was infinitely moving. 'My darling, you mean that?'

She gazed at him as if in a trance. Had she only imagined the implication in the endearment, in the look in his eyes and the sound of his voice? And then his arms were around her and his lips were on hers, demanding, passionate, staking a claim to which she had given him every right, and there was no imagining the depth of his desire.

'I wondered sometimes if I was was mad to urge Mary and George to take a holiday,' Nicholas said a little later, as he caressed the tumble of curls which lay against his chest, bare where the buttons of his shirt had been parted.

'A holiday?' Kelly jerked upright, her eyes wide and startled.

'George was discharged from hospital two weeks ago. He could have come back then, but I ordered Mary to take him off to the sea to recuperate.'

'Why?' Kelly stared up into the stern features of the man she loved more than she had ever thought possible.

'To give you time to get to know me. To realise your engagement to Gary was a mistake.'

'I'm not engaged. I haven't been for days.' A quick movement and then the ring was off her finger. 'But Nicholas, what about Serena?'

'The kiss you saw was a goodbye. After the day we spent together at Pinevale, I knew that I had to have you with me always. Serena came for supper and later we had a long talk.'

'Was that why you were so distant?'

His eyes narrowed slightly. 'You noticed?'

'Noticed?' A small sob escaped her. 'I couldn't understand what had happened. I . . . I was so hurt.'

'For the last time,' he promised. 'Kelly, you'd turned my world upside down. You weren't the girl I'd imagined. And I loved you so much. I had to think, come to terms with it all . . .'

'Oh, Nicholas! Darling . . . have I been very foolish?'

'Very. But so was I.' Strong arms drew her back on to his chest, and his lips probed a bare shoulder. 'I love you, Kelly. And I want you. And the Andersons need their bedroom back. When will you marry me?'

'Next week?' she ventured mischievously.

'Tomorrow,' he said firmly. There was no time to argue the point as strong lips pressed down on hers. And moments later any wish to talk had vanished.

What readers say about Harlequin Presents

"Harlequin books are so refreshing that they take you into a different world with each one you read."

D.L.,* Jacksboro, Texas

"I hope Harlequin goes on forever."

M.Z., Hollywood, California

"Harlequin books are great; once you start reading them, you always want to read more."

T.E., Ogden, Utah

"Harlequin books bring love, happiness and romance into my very routine life."

N.J., Springfield, Missouri

*Names available on request

Harlequin Presents...

The books that let you escape into the wonderful world of romance! Trips to exotic places... interesting plots... meeting memorable people... the excitement of love.... These are integral parts of Harlequin Presents— the heartwarming novels read by women everywhere.

Many early issues are now available. Choose from this great selection!

Choose from this list of Harlequin Presents editions

165	The Arrogance of Love	Anne Mather
166	Familiar Stranger	Lilian Peake
158	Dangerous Friendship	Anne Hampson
169	Cupboard Love	Roberta Leigh
170	The High Valley	Anne Mather
172	Roman Affair	Rachel Lindsay
173	Valley Deep, Mountain High	Anne Mather
174	The Burning Sands	Violet Winspear
175	Man without a Heart	Roberta Leigh
176	Tinsel Star	Rachel Lindsay
177	Smouldering Flame	Anne Mather
178	The Sun Tower	Violet Winspear
179	Sanctuary in the Desert	Elizabeth Ashton
181	Isle at the Rainbow's End	Anne Hampson
182	Unwilling Bridegroom	Roberta Leigh
183	Valley of the Vapours	Janet Dailey
184	A Man to Tame	Rachel Lindsay
185	Wild Enchantress	Anne Mather
186	A Bitter Loving	Lilian Peake
187	Hills of Kalamata	Anne Hampson
188	The Marquis Takes a Wife	Rachel Lindsay
189	Beware the Beast	Anne Mather
190	This Man Her Enemy	Lilian Peake
191	Strange Adventure	Sara Craven

Relive a great romance...
Harlequin Presents 1980
Complete and mail this coupon today!

Harlequin Reader Service

In U.S.A.
MPO Box 707
Niagara Falls, N.Y. 14302

In Canada
649 Ontario St.
Stratford, Ontario, N5A 6W2

Please send me the following Harlequin Presents novels. I am enclosing my check or money order for $1.50 for each novel ordered, plus 59¢ to cover postage and handling.

☐ 165	☐ 175	☐ 184
☐ 166	☐ 176	☐ 185
☐ 168	☐ 177	☐ 186
☐ 169	☐ 178	☐ 187
☐ 170	☐ 179	☐ 188
☐ 172	☐ 181	☐ 189
☐ 173	☐ 182	☐ 190
☐ 174	☐ 183	☐ 191

Number of novels checked @ $1.50 each = $_____

N.Y. State residents add appropriate sales tax $_____

Postage and handling $_____.59

TOTAL $_____

I enclose _____
(Please send check or money order. We cannot be responsible for cash sent through the mail.)

Prices subject to change without notice.

NAME _____
(Please Print)

ADDRESS _____

CITY _____

STATE/PROV. _____

ZIP/POSTAL CODE _____

Offer expires December 31, 1980.

0065631